Yes, Captain

Sierra Shipley

Cover Design by Sierra Shipley

Table of Contents

Books By Sierra

The Claiming Her Series

His Temptation

His Disaster

His Reward

His Challenge

The Rose Prairie Series

All Tangled Up

Tied In Nots

It Had To Be You

Interconnected Stand Alone

Yes, Captain

Hey, Neighbor

The Single Dads Club

Loved by the Single Dad

Nanny for the Single Dad

Desired by the Single Dad

SIERRA SHIPLEY

Prologue

Hannah

Another day, another adventure. At least, not until tomorrow. Tonight, we party. I might be hungover for my first day back on the boat, but who cares? No one can deny a twenty-three-year-old her fun, right?

It's the night before I spend my third summer on board the motor yacht *Siren* as the one and only stewardess for the owners, Dr. and Mr. Olivier. Several years ago during summer break from college, they learned I was looking for a job from my mother. I was lucky enough to have grown up playing in their gigantic backyard after school while my mom finished her daily duties as their housekeeper, so they offered me a position on their yacht for the summer. It's not every day that a daughter of a housekeeper and an electrician gets a job on a luxury yacht, so I jumped at the opportunity and never looked back.

Growing up in Fort Lauderdale surrounded by big white boats with the ocean out your front door, adventure practically calls to you, and I was no exception. Sure, I went to college to appease my parents, but my heart longs to see the world. Mom wasn't thrilled when I followed her footsteps and became a glorified maid on a boat, but I think of all the possibilities a job like this offers: fun, money, and adventure.

Since that first summer, I've traveled to many places I've only dreamed of seeing working as a stewardess hopping from boat to boat. Now, I'm finding myself back where I started, and I wouldn't have it any other way. The Oliviers are amazing and working with them is more relaxed than during a normal charter season.

Let's just call this my "vacation". If you call working on a 40-meter yacht, cleaning all day, every day, and serving others a vacation.

"Hannah!" An accompanying bang on the bathroom door momentarily startles me, almost making me ruin my makeup. "Hurry your ass up!"

Not feeling one ounce of urgency, I take my time to fluff my chestnut tresses, the curls falling into soft waves flowing to my waist. Tiffany can bang on the door all she wants, but I'm taking my time.

Tiff and I met on my first charter after leaving motor yacht *Siren*. She worked as the second stewardess while I was the third. After spending six weeks together, we'd grown so close that it made sense for us to move in together during the off-season.

She's the Christina to my Meredith, or whatever.

By the time I open the bathroom door, I look pretty damn close to perfect. The yellow dress hugs my tits and ass, making them appear more juicy than normal. They're really just normal boobs, but tonight they look amazing. I went with a more minimal look when it came to my make-up, making my blue eyes seem bigger with neutral tones.

I feel hot as hell.

Tiff is perched on the couch with her eyes on her phone when I emerge from the bathroom. "I'm ready for my close-up," I croon dramatically while leaning against the corner and doing a little shimmy.

It should be noted that I don't act like this with everyone. Do I like to have fun? Absolutely. Do I always act like one of those party bimbos? No. Except for tonight. A girl has to have her exceptions, right? Otherwise, where would all the fun go?

Tiff rolls her brown eyes at me and pushes herself up onto her way too-tall heels, which I know are going to end up with me carrying them—and her—when we head home. "Finally, bitch. Let's go."

When she gets close enough, I grab her around her waist pulling her close as we walk arm-in-arm out the front door. "You know you love me," I tease, leaning in and pressing a quick peck to her cheek.

"God, you're ridiculous," she laughs, playfully swiping away remnants of my lip gloss. "C'mon, Han. Let's celebrate your last night of freedom."

And fuck, do we ever.

Chapter One

Hannah

The morning sunlight beams its rays straight into my goddamn corneas. Blinding pain seems to spear into my still-hungover brain making me wince. I knew this was going to happen, but last night I didn't care.

I sure as shit care now.

Every flicker of light off the water sends a sharp pain to my eyes that even my stylish sunglasses can't block.

Tiff and I had taken shot after shot last night and danced until my feet felt like they were going to fall off. If you're going to be a yachty, you've gotta party like one. But damn, am I paying for it today.

Dragging my bag behind me down the dock I try in vain to block the killer rays from frying my brain. Reaching up, I tug my floppy hat lower on my brow and block the sun with my hand just as a giant gust of wind blows right into me, making my white sundress rise over my waist. The sun hat perched on my head attempts to fly away, the floppy sides flapping in the wind threatening to take off while simultaneously slapping me in the face. An embarrassingly girly squeal squeaks its way out of my mouth as I fight the wind.

I would normally turn this into a graceful Marilyn Monroe-esque moment, but my hungover brain panics.

Shit, shit, shit.

My right hand covering my eyes reaches for my hat, holding the slapping thing in place, but for some reason, I can't seem to work both my hands at the same damn time. My left

7

hand must be superglued to the handle of my luggage for all the good it does to help keep my dress down, which is none. The flowing skirt swirls up my thighs, no doubt revealing my underwear to whoever happens to be looking.

Finally, it seems my muddled brain sends the signal to my hand to let go and I'm able to pry my grip free from the handle. My left-hand slams down on the flyaway skirt pinning what I can to my upper thigh, saving a bit of my modesty. My ass cheeks are most definitely making their appearance, the breeze gracing places that shouldn't feel a breeze, but there's nothing I can do about that now.

What a way to start off the day.

"Oh my god, oh my god, oh my god," I repeat my mantra frozen in place until the gust of wind settles. But then the sound of my bag rolling across the concrete walkway of the dock gets my attention. "Shit," I curse, unable to do anything to stop it unless I'm willing to flash the entire port again.

Which I am not.

This better not be the universe's way of telling me that shits about to go down, 'cause I ain't having it. I'm here to have three weeks of a peaceful charter with the most chill owners I've ever met. It's my mother freaking time to reset and I'm not going to let anything ruin it.

One of the best things about working for Dr. and Mr. Olivier is that they are so sweet and kind. Having spent the last several years working on yachts, I've seen my fair share of high-maintenance guests and know a good thing when I see it. Maybe it's because I've known them most of my life and they're old enough to be my grandparents that I'm a little biased.

YES, CAPTAIN

Let's just say that going from their yacht into my first charting season was a whirlwind.

Yachting is something that's always been part of my life. On weekends, my dad would take me to the marina to look at the '"big white boats." We'd spot our favorites and laugh at their names before getting ice cream. Just thinking about it makes me cry. Those are treasured memories. Ones that will never be made again.

Right before I left for my first charter yacht, Dad died suddenly of a heart attack. Everything at that moment stopped. The world quit spinning because to Mom and me, it did.

The wind settles after several moments and I'm able to try to smooth down my skirt and secure my hat on my head before searching for my bag. Luckily it didn't go far, but it fell over, the end of it dangerously hanging over the edge of the dock. I watch in horror as a new gust of wind makes my luggage wobble, and I lunge. My knees hit painfully against the concrete of the dock, my arms reaching for my bag before it tumbles into the waves below.

I can't believe I fucking caught it.

Now that would be one helluva way to start the summer.

Straightening my shoulders and doing my best to not look hungover, I walk down the dock to the *Siren*. She's not the largest yacht I've been on, but she holds a special place in my heart. I know every nook and cranny of her and stepping onto her deck will be like coming home.

Stopping at the gangway of the boat, I kick off my sandals, bending over to pick them up and examining my scraped knees. Thankfully they aren't scraped up too bad and blood isn't dripping down my knees, so I see that as a win. Taking careful steps I manage to hit the teak of the swim platform with a sigh of relief. There's no one here to greet me, but that's not all that unusual.

The main deck of the yacht has the aft deck with sunny seating and amazing views of the water, including a swim platform for when the guests want to take a dip. The boat looks relatively clean and taken care of, which is good for me.

Stepping into the main salon through the recessed glass doors, the cool air of the interior hits me. It never ceases to amaze me how luxurious it all is. Windows on the port and starboard sides of the boat light up the interior, and the skylights over the formal dining area are one of my favorite features.

Breathing in the cool air, I remove my hat and gently set it on top of my bag. The first stop, once you get on the boat is to see the captain and I know just where he is.

Captain Lewis is an amazing older gentleman who holds a special place in my heart. By far, he's the favorite captain I've ever had. The Oliviers have employed him for years and I can't wait to see him.

Finding the spiral stairs off the galley, I practically skip up to the bridge. "Hey, Cap!" I call the moment my foot hits the top step. Just picturing his crinkly face and toothy grin has me beaming.

Rounding the corner to the bridge, I stop in my tracks, my smile fading from my face. My favorite wrinkled and wise captain isn't the one sitting in the captain's chair.

"From now on, it's Captain."

The deep voice of the stranger sitting in the seat is smooth like honey, sending a delicious shiver down my spine. He swivels the seat to face me and I swear to god I stop breathing. He's the sexiest man I think I've ever seen in real life, and trust me, I've seen some sexy men while on charter. His blue eyes skewer me in place and I'm frozen. It's amazing I'm not drooling at this point.

"Understood?"

Trying to hide my shock, I blink rapidly sucking in discreet breaths to try to even my skyrocketing heart rate. "Yes, Captain."

I manage to at least not sound like a complete idiot, but honestly what girl wouldn't be struck dumb looking at this man? He's got long, strong legs, a trim waist from what I can see, and large broad shoulders attached to some seriously strong arms. And *oh my god*, his face is glorious too with a strong jaw, lush lips, and eyes the color of a clear day at sea.

Somehow I remember my manners, stepping further into the room and offering my manicured hand to him. "Hannah Carper, the stewardess. It's nice to meet you."

He doesn't stand but politely takes my hand in his, squeezing it tightly in his large grasp. "Captain Pike. Nice to meet you, Hannah."

Nervously I glance around the bridge focusing on anything but the man in front of me. The bridge is the command center of the ship with sonar and radar readings displayed on the many screens. Behind me is a small booth and built-in shelves with various notebooks that I assume contain important information. To the left is a door leading to the gangway on the side of the ship making it easy to access the decks.

"Um, sorry for that," I gesture over my shoulder toward the top of the steps. "I was expecting Captain Lewis, is he doing okay?" As dumbstruck as I am about seeing this adonis in front of me, my heart still worries about Captain Lewis.

Captain Pike releases my hand and nods. "He decided to retire this year. Did his final walkthrough with me last week."

"Oh, well, good for him," I stammer as I force a smile on my face and try to seem upbeat. "I'll just go and set up for the rest of the crew since I'm the first one here." I turn and reach the top of the steps when his voice stops me.

"I look forward to working with you, Hannah." Turning, I look over at him still sitting in the captain's chair. His dirty blond hair has streaks of gray on his temples making it clear that he is without a doubt, too old for me.

Smiling, I nod my head in agreement. "Captain."

Chapter Two

Anson

S crewed. Utterly and completely screwed.

Of course, the beautiful woman I couldn't take my eyes off of as she walked down the dock is on this ship. I thought I'd died and gone to heaven when she struggled to keep her dress down showcasing those beautiful, mouthwatering legs.

Completely off-limits.

She's quite possibly the most beautiful woman I've ever seen. Her chestnut hair is pulled back into a ponytail hanging down to her trim waist. That motherfucking sundress had my mouth watering and dick hard the instant I turned around making it impossible for me to stand or else face a sexual harassment charge.

Hannah. Her name rings like a gong through my mind. Hannah with those blue eyes that shine like the Caribbean.

Fuck, I'm so screwed.

Not only is she off-limits, but she's also too damn young for me. I have to be at least a decade older than her, my hair and beard already flecked with gray.

The number one rule of yachting is 'don't screw the crew' and I've never been as tempted as I am right now. Back in my younger days, sure, I had my fun, but never since I climbed my way up the chain of command.

Fuck.

This job is supposed to be a means to an end. A final hurrah before buying my own boat and traveling the world. I've been a captain for a long damn time, traveling through exquisite waters and seeing breathtaking views, but never on my own boat.

I can't make Hannah a distraction. I don't need a distraction.

But maybe I want one...

Shit, I can't think this way. She's *not* an option. Somehow, I know I'm fighting a losing battle, but damn if I don't try.

Footsteps coming up the stairs pull me from my internal hell. The crew of the *Siren* arrive today to ready the boat before the owners come tomorrow. Not having a continual turnover of guests should make for a more relaxed summer season. That's if the weather stays calm, but there's no telling what can happen.

"Captain?" Standing before me is a tall guy with a serious, focused expression on his face. He holds out his hand in greeting, "I'm Garrett, your first mate."

I remember looking at his CV and finding him highly qualified. He's risen from deckhand to first mate quickly. I can tell he's going to go above and beyond on this job, clearly having captain as his next goal.

My body finally calm after seeing Hannah up close, I stand, grasping his hand. "Right. Nice to meet you, Garrett. It looks like you've got a lot of experience."

He sucks in a deep breath as he scans the bridge and out the windows. "Yes, sir. I was on a 90-meter last season as a bosun and earned my stripes. Don't worry, I have all the certifications and plan on doing my best."

He's so eager that I can't help but grin at him. "I can see that." Crossing over to the stack of files, I hand him the one on the top. "Here is your deck crew. You can pick for yourself who will be bosun. The stewardess, Hanah, is already on board. She'll have your uniform and room assignment."

Garrett flips through the file, nodding his head as he does. "Thanks, Captain. I'll let you know when I make my choice." Then with a quick nod, he leaves.

Several hours later the rest of the crew arrived and make their introductions. Since the *Siren* is 40 meters and small compared to superyachts, we have a minimal crew. One stewardess, a first mate, a bosun, two deck crew, and an engineer. Honestly, it feels more like a skeleton crew, but the owners like it this way.

Stepping free of the bridge, the salty sea air fills my nostrils. Closing my eyes I take a moment to bathe in the warm sun, centering myself on the job at hand. Friendly chatter of the crew carries across the boat as the deck crew scrubs it down and I do my best to ignore it, but a hushed feminine voice filters over to me, making me pause.

"So, is there anyone on board who you find attractive?" Her question is met with a deep, male chuckle.

"I'm not sure yet."

"Oh c'mon," the girl laughs. "There's gotta be someone you're interested in. What's your type?"

This shit always happens on boats. All these young, attractive free-spirits gathered in one place, hook-ups are bound to happen. I don't think the female voice is Hannah, but I have to know. There's only one other female crew member on board and that's Keeran.

Sneaking across the bow, I turn the corner onto the aft deck where they're working, their backs to me keeping me hidden.

"Well, my only options are you and Hannah and you're both fucking fine as hell."

"Completely straight, huh? Garrett's pretty hot." Keeran has her blond hair braided to one side as she and Robbie talk and work. She shoots him a smile and a wink before turning back to her work, making him laugh.

I've heard enough.

"How's it going?" Both jump in surprise at the sound of my voice. Robbie straightens, brushing his hair off his forehead and Keeran's eyes go wide.

"Hey, Captain. We're getting it done." Robbie, at least I think that's his name, tips his head in my direction and gets back to cleaning the boat.

"Good." Underneath us, I can hear shuffling coming from the tender garage where Garrett and Aiden are working to sort through the various water toys. "Make sure you're hitting the stainless," I instruct before leaving them behind.

The doors to the main salon open and I see Hannah kneeling on the floor, ass in the air, as she digs through a cabinet. Her gray standard-issue skirt is tight across her ass, leaving little to the imagination.

How in the hell am I going to stay away from her?

My jaw clenches rhythmically as I stride straight on through to the galley. It's amazing that I was even able to pull my gaze away from the feast that was in front of me.

She really is going to make this impossible.

With a sigh, I grab the radio fob hanging from my ear and bring it to my lips and push on the button to speak. "All crew, all crew. Meet me in the sky lounge in five minutes." It's about time for the crew to learn my expectations and management style.

The sky lounge is located on the top section of the boat. It has a closed-in seating area large enough to fit all the crew members. The entire back wall is floor-to-ceiling windows that lead out to a deck with plush seating for the guests to enjoy the sunshine. The *Siren* may be small, but she doesn't lack in luxury.

Everyone's waiting for me in the sky lounge and it takes all my willpower to keep my eyes from focusing on Hannah. She's so damn beautiful. She's pulled her long hair over one shoulder and her cheeks are flushed pink, either from working or from seeing me.

I'm not ignorant of the effect I tend to have on women and I noticed how she looked at me when we first met.

You can stare at me all you want, Hannah.

"Welcome to motor yacht *Siren*. I wanted to take a minute to speak to you all as a crew. Trust is earned with me, and you'll have to work hard for it. You all know how to do your jobs, but that doesn't mean I trust you to do them well—at least not yet." Several crew members swallow hard, others nod their heads. Not Hannah though. She sits up and squares her shoulders.

Interesting.

"Our main priority while on charter is safety for everyone on board. From what I'm told, the Oliviers will have guests from time to time, so Hannah," I gesture towards the lone stewardess, "might need some help. We are a team and will work as such. If you keep all those in mind, we'll have a great season."

"Now, let me introduce you to our chief engineer and first mate." The two men sit to my left, separate from the crew. "Joe here," the older, balding man waves at the crew sitting across from him, "is our engineer. If anyone needs help with anything, he's your guy."

"Our first mate, Garrett." Garrett nods his head. "He'll be in charge of the deck crew and help oversee the bridge." I find myself checking in with Hannah like I could see whether she finds him attractive or not. Ever since I heard Keeran say she thought he was attractive I couldn't help but wonder if Hannah agrees. He's more age-appropriate, that's for sure.

"If I may, Captain?" Chef Damon leans forward from his spot on the couch and I nod for him to continue. "All that I ask is that you keep the galley clear from any clutter. If you have any requests for crew food, just let me know."

Shit, how did I not notice the British accent? Keeran is practically drooling, and Hannah has glassy eyes listening to him talk.

The fact that I'm finding myself jealous of a woman who I barely know is not good for my resolve. I just wonder how long I'll be able to hold out.

Chapter Three

It might be just me, but this entire crew is ridiculously attractive. We've got a captain who is hot as sin, and a first officer who could give Captain America a run for his money. There's sexy Robbie with his silky dark hair that flops in his eyes, Aidan who has this boy next door look, and Keeran with her gorgeous sun-streaked blond hair and bronzed skin. Don't even get me started on Chef Damon because I might literally swoon. Swoon! I feel like the ugly duckling of the bunch.

My radio crackles with static before Damon's voice filters through. "Hannah, can you meet me in the galley?" God, he even sounds good over the freaking radio.

Putting the container back on the shelf in the pantry, I search for the earpiece of the radio dangling from my shirt collar. "Yep. I'll be there in a minute."

One thing that took a little getting used to is the radio. I had one captain who would steal a radio if he found one sitting out, and you did *not* want that to happen. I learned that lesson quickly and ever since, I constantly check for my radio. It's just like me to set something down and forget all about it.

Which I did.

Many times.

The galley, or the kitchen, is a tight space on the port side of the main salon. It's all stainless steel and top-of-the-line appliances. Windows are spaced evenly along the outside wall allowing for some sunlight to filter through illuminating the space. There's a small walkway leading from the door to the stairs that head up to the bridge, each side blocked in with counters stocked with all types of gadgets. On the other side of the counters is the chef's workspace complete with a sink, stove, grill... You name it, it's there.

"Oh cheffy," I sing as I walk through the doorway of the galley. Damon's sifting through the fridges, no doubt checking the produce left over from the previous charter. Most yachts are rented out during charter seasons when the owners have no use for them and when the crew leaves, food is left behind for the next chef to sift through.

"Hello, beautiful." He leans around the door of the fridge giving me a flirtatious smile. He's going to be so much fun; I can already tell.

"Ooh, a girl could get used to that." Leaning my hip on the counter I cross my arms under my chest and smile at him giving him a playful wink. The flirting is all fun and games. He's gorgeous, but not for me. My type at the moment is the chiseled, super-sexy captain. "What did you need me for?"

"Well alright then," he grins at me as he closes the door and braces his elbows on the counter, linking his hands together. "Rumor has it you know the owners." I nod my head making an mm-hmm sound in my throat as he talks. "I was wondering if you could give me some insight into their likes and dislikes."

"Sure thing." I've already taped up their preferences on the cabinet across from me, and I scan through them, my finger tapping my chin. Glancing through the list, I share what I know about Grace and Mark while he asks me questions. Damon seems very particular and a perfectionist, so his questions are thorough.

"Thank you, that's helpful. You're a doll." He winks playfully at me before turning back to the fridge.

Pushing myself off the counter, I turn for the door, calling over my shoulder, "You bet." But as soon as the words leave my mouth, I run smack into a strong chest. "Oh my gosh, I'm so sorry!" Stepping back, I look up to see Captain Pike's blue eyes staring down at me.

He's just so...intimidating. He has this dominant, rugged air about him that makes my heart flutter uncontrollably in my chest.

His hands wrap around the top of my arms as he steps to the side to let me through. "It's alright. Just be more careful."

I suck in a too-ragged breath, giving him a tight smile. "Yes, Captain," I mutter before stepping through the short hallway and back onto the main salon.

Now that I'm out of sight, I have to fan my too-hot face. I've got to pull myself together, or this charter is going to be hell.

Keeran opens the glass doors from the aft deck and eyes me suspiciously.

"What the heck happened to you?" she asks, her voice a whisper, her face practically begging for juicy gossip. We're the only two girls on board making us roommates and the only person I can girl talk with.

My eyes scan the empty room and I shake my head. There are too many places for people to overhear our conversation and the last thing I need is for a rumor to spread.

"Come here." Grabbing her arm, I drag her down the steps to the crew area and straight to our tiny room.

Yachts are amazing places for people with too much money to enjoy themselves while the crew is shoved below deck in tiny living quarters. We pass through the small crew mess that consists of a booth and kitchenette, the cabinets stocked with snacks. On either side of the crew mess is a long, skinny hallway. Down one end is the door to the engine room and laundry room where I will no doubt be spending plenty of time. The other end of the hallway has rooms for the crew bunks.

The rooms they shove us in are tiny, but if you think about it, we're all so busy working that all we do during our downtime is sleep, so they don't have to be gigantic. Each room has a bunk bed, two tiny closets, and a small bathroom with a standing shower that feels more like a coffin that's barely big enough to turn around in.

Once in our room, Keeran sits on my bottom bunk, and I join her, plopping down with a sigh. Grabbing my penguin Squishmallow, I hug it tight to my chest. It's the last gift my dad ever gave me and there's no way I could leave Henry behind.

"Spill." Keeran's face is eager with excitement.

"Are we in heaven? I mean, have you seen the men on this boat?" Keeran laughs and nods her head.

"Bitch, we must be because oh my god!" She's busy fanning her face and dramatically panting. "I was trying to get a feel of what the guys were thinking about us but got non-answers."

"So, who are you crushing on?" There's bound to be a 'boat-mance' and it's not going to be me, so my money is on Keeran.

"Robbie," she swoons, dramatically falling against the mattress. "There's just something about him."

YES, CAPTAIN

When I think of a yachty, Robbie is who I picture. He's got this go-with-the-flow type attitude that draws people in. I can totally see why Keeran's crushing hard for him. I mean, Robbie is gorgeous. His jet black curly hair constantly flops over his forehead blocking his dark brown eyes that seem to always be twinkling with amusement.

"I say you should go for it. Who doesn't love a bit of drama?"

She scoffs and waves me off. "I don't know. We'll see. But now it's your turn. Who has you all hot and bothered?"

Hmmm, decisions, decisions. Do I tell Keeran about my instant attraction to Captain Pike, or do I keep my mouth shut? But now that I think about it, there's no way I'll be able to keep it hidden from her, so I might as well tell her. It's only a crush. Nothing is going to happen.

"You have to swear to secrecy." I make a show of looking her dead in the eyes. "You can't tell anyone."

Keeran mimes locking her lips, a smile pulling at the corners.

"Alright," I breathe, trying to force my nerves down and squaring my shoulders. "I've kind of got a thing for Captain."

"Pfft," she scoffs, arranging her legs underneath her. "Who the fuck doesn't have a thing for him? For real, this whole damn boat is filled with the world's hottest men and the captain is their leader." We both break out into a fit of giggles. "I say," she huffs, "if you get the chance to ride that dick you take it. Then come and tell me all about it!"

Part of me has serious doubts that he has any interest in me. I mean, the man barely looked at me and couldn't be bothered to stand and greet me like a gentleman.

But hell, I wouldn't turn him down if he offered.

We talk our way through the other crew members, sharing what we know about them so far, but after our quick gossip session, it's back to work. The boat might be in good condition after the previous charter season, but there's still a lot to do and I'm the only one to do it.

I've checked and organized the cabinets to my liking, cleaned the day heads, started the laundry for the guest bedding, and now I'm cleaning the guest rooms.

All with a fucking hangover.

Thankfully after downing several water bottles and popping some headache medicine the sharp ache has faded into a dull one.

Note to self, don't show up to work hungover. It makes everything a thousand times more difficult.

It's getting late, the sun beginning to set through the windows as I work casting the room in an orange glow. Garrett already came on the radio telling the deck crew to go down for the night and to be on deck early in the morning, but I know I'm not getting sleep anytime soon. With the Oliviers arriving tomorrow and all this work still left to do, I have a feeling it's going to be a long night.

One thing I enjoy about my job is the quiet solitude. There's something therapeutic about changing the sheets, wiping down counters, and scrubbing toilets. I'm not saying that it's fun or even enjoyable, but the repetitive motions are soothing.

After a while of working in pleasant silence, I slide my headphones over my head and get to work. I fear if I don't give myself something to listen to, I'll fall asleep on the bed I'm attempting to make. My thumb slides through all my Spotify playlists before settling on one and letting the music blast. It doesn't take long for my hips to sway to the beat as I putz around the room. It was a smart choice because I'm already feeling more awake.

Out of nowhere, a tap on my shoulder has me yelp in fright. My hand flies to my headphones, ripping them off my head.

"How are you handling everything?" Captain Pike's deep voice makes me jump. Again. I'm fitting the sheets in the owner's suite and look up to find him standing behind me, leaning against the wall.

Why is that so damn attractive? Maybe it's that dominance thing but I like the feeling of him towering over me. Maybe I like it too much...

"Sorry," I gasp, my hand over my pounding heart. "You scared me." He doesn't say anything, just crosses his arms over that delicious chest of his. "Um, everything's great. Keeping me busy," I chuckle.

His eyes travel around the room before landing on me. "What do you need help with?"

Why is he asking me this? Most captains trust that their crew will get things done, but hadn't he already said his trust has to be earned?

I think for a moment while I smooth out the sheets. "I'm making the beds now, but the vacuuming needs to be done." More than that needs to be done really, but I'm not telling him that.

He gives a brisk nod of his head and unwinds his arms. "If you need anything, just let me know. Don't worry about vacuuming. I've got it."

"No, it's okay—" I protest, but he cuts me off.

"Hannah." He says my name in a way that's both comforting and demanding.

"Yes, Captain?" I swallow hard and meet his gaze.

"I've got you, Hannah." Those sky-blue eyes of his have my insides turning molten and his words make my muscles clench. He gives me a warm smile and a pointed look before leaving me.

This crush is going to make this charter impossible.

Chapter Four

Anson

W hat the fuck am I doing?

The only thing on this motherfucking boat that's a siren is Hannah. Everything she does calls to me.

When I went down to the crew mess for dinner and saw everyone there but Hannah, I couldn't stop my feet from moving to find her. I like to think that I'm being a good captain and helping her out, but that's far from the truth. I want to be near her.

Pathetic.

She had been dancing as she worked and like a creep, I stood right outside the door watching. I couldn't take my eyes off the swing of her hips and the roundness of her ass.

Hannah does have a lot on her hands and if I can do something as simple as vacuuming to ease her load, then I'll do it. But I'll do more than vacuum. I caught the little lie the moment the words left her mouth, that adorable nose of hers scrunching as she lied. As I walk through the boat, I spotted some things I could do to help her and quickly found the cleaning supplies I needed. It's not much, but every little bit helps.

The hum of the vacuum leaves me alone with my thoughts and all I can focus on is the way that pretty mouth of hers says captain. It makes my dick twitch and I want to hear it again.

I'm playing with fire and we haven't even left the dock. Once again I find myself clenching my teeth at the thought of having to keep my distance.

A distance that is growing more impossible to keep.

By the time I slide into the sheets of the Captain's quarters, I'm exhausted, but nothing can stop my mind from thinking of her. Of how Hannah's probably curled up in her bunk down below, all alone in that bed of hers. My mind strays to other impossible and improbable things, like how her skin would feel under my hands, and the warmth of her body next to mine. These thoughts plague my mind, unable to let me drift off into the peaceful oblivion of sleep.

Before I know it, the sun is rising above the horizon signaling a new day and it feels as if I barely slept.

Working on yachts has made me an early riser and nothing will change that, even a shitty night's sleep.

Making my way down the steps and into the galley, I'm surprised to find Hannah already up. Our guests don't arrive until later this morning and there's no need for her to be awake right now, especially at the ass-crack of dawn.

"Good morning." My voice is still gruff from sleep and I fight the urge to clear my throat. She's got on her uniform, the red *Siren* shirt and gray skirt, her pen tapping against her lower lip as she leans on the counter, a pad of paper in front of her.

Hannah turns to me and I can't help but notice her sharp intake of breath. "Good morning, Captain. Is there anything I can get you?" She straightens, fidgeting with the hem of her skirt.

It's so early that even Damon isn't up working in the galley and the thought that we're alone together thrills me.

"No, it's alright. Don't worry about me." Playfully I nudge her shoulder as I pass by her for the coffee needing to touch her, and I'm rewarded with a soft smile. She must have already brewed a pot and I notice the steaming mug in front of her that looks more like cream than coffee. "Long night?" I ask nodding towards her mug.

She nods her head stifling a yawn. "Oh, you know, there's always more work to be done."

Absently I wonder just how long she stayed up and what I would have done if I'd known. Would I have helped her more if I had? Part of me says I wouldn't have been able to stop myself.

I don't say anything, pouring myself a cup of black coffee and taking a sip. Out of the corner of my eye, Hannah reaches for her mug, lifting it off the counter by the rim. I watch as the mug slips through her fingers, shattering on the floor with its impact, the sound of breaking glass cutting through the sleepy quiet of the boat.

"Shit," she curses, carefully stepping away from the broken shards, her feet bare and unprotected. Unable to bear the thought of her being hurt, my hands settle around her waist, and I pull her behind me, away from the glass.

"Don't move," I say, my voice coming out harsh.

"I'm sorry, Captain." I bend down to pick up the broken shards and see her shuffling her feet. "Here, let me go get a rag and help you."

"No, you won't. You're going to stay right there," I order. "I don't want you to hurt yourself." Can this girl not follow orders?

That's something I'll have to remedy.

Fuck. No.

My palm itches with the image of her ass draped across my lap, her cheeks red and tender. No matter what, I can't let that happen. But I want it to. I want her full submission, her obedience, her tied up and wet for me.

Shut. It. Down.

"It's not a problem," she chuckles as if she had a funny thought. "With the number of glasses I break, I'm a pro cleaner by now."

Then, she completely defies my order by stepping around my hunched frame as I scan the floor for any remaining shards. The retort dies in my throat the moment she gasps in pain.

"Ouch. Oh shit." She balances on one leg teetering between my back and the counter and grabs my shoulder to steady herself making my whole body freeze at the innocent contact.

The image of that hand caressing my cock forms instantly in my mind.

I can't think of that right now.

Transferring the broken shards to my left hand, I grab her hip with my right and stand, depositing the shards on the counter. Without thinking my palms settle on the curve of her ass, lifting her onto the counter in one swift move.

At that movement the entire atmosphere shifts. Her eyes are wide, and her breathing is heavy. I'm planted between her parted thighs, all thought of her injury gone. Our gazes lock, neither one daring to look away as time freezes, our souls connecting like we've found our missing halves.

Hannah swallows hard before whispering, "My foot..."

For a moment, I'm confused. "Your foot? Right." Crouching in front of her, I take her leg in my hands to inspect her injury. My palm glides down her soft, smooth skin, noticing small scrapes on her knee before stopping at her ankle. Goosebumps pop up along her skin, but she doesn't shy away from my touch, her breath quickening. The feel of her skin under my touch makes it difficult to concentrate, but the sight of her bleeding has me gritting my teeth. The small shard of glass sticks out of her heel, the blood beginning to flow down the sole of her foot.

Hannah stiffens a moment before a voice cuts in. "Well, well, well. What do we have here?" Damon leans against the galley door, his eyebrows arched.

"I'm glad you're here," I say, not all that disappointed that he's interrupting, especially when Hannah is hurting. "I need you to go get the med kit. Hannah stepped on some glass."

Damon turns and calls over his shoulder, "On it."

Standing I scan the galley for paper towels before unspooling a few, some for the spilled coffee, the other to keep her blood from dripping on the floor.

"I should've known I'd find the last piece of glass with my foot. Typical." She sits still while I kneel before her, cleaning her foot the best I can.

"Do you do this often?" I tease, genuinely curious.

She shrugs. "I'm accident-prone. It was bound to happen eventually." Heavy footsteps pound up the stairs from the crew quarters.

"Got it." Damon sets the med kit on the counter next to Hannah. "I'll clean up the spill."

"Just be mindful of the glass on the counter. Once I'm done with this," I nudge my head at Hannah's foot, "I'll get out the vacuum."

"You guys don't have to do this," Hannah pleads. "It's my fault and I can clean it up. Seriously, just let me do it."

Both Damon and I say no at the same time, making Hannah throw her hands up in frustration.

"Oh my god," she mumbles under her breath. "You two are impossible."

If she only knew.

I take my time cleaning her foot, carefully pulling the shard from her skin with barely a hiss from her. "There, all done. Try to be careful this time," I order, as she slides down off the counter carefully testing her newly bandaged foot.

She smiles sweetly at me, her voice singsong as she says, "No promises."

This girl is going to drive me crazy, and now that I know the feel of her skin brushing against mine, I fear nothing will stand in my way from feeling it again.

Chapter Five

Hannah

My heel is still tender as I walk on it, but there's a job to do.

Last night, I worked until the early hours of the morning sorting out the provisions that still needed unloading from the afternoon delivery. The stew pantry quickly filled up with the order which meant I had to get creative, finding open storage anywhere I could. It took longer than I expected.

Since Captain won't let me clean up my own mess—the sexy bastard—I pour a new mug of coffee and grab my pad of paper. The list of things to do had grown the longer I stood there, so as odd as it sounds, I was kind of glad for the distraction, even if it meant I hurt myself.

Captain Pike is impossibly sexier today than he was yesterday, which I didn't even know that's a thing, but apparently, it is. It also didn't help that he was between my thighs and caressing my skin. As a matter of fact, I might need to change my panties because surely the ones I'm wearing are ruined. The combination of his hands gripping my ass and him kneeling in front of me practically had me panting.

Ugh, I have to stop with these thoughts. It's. Never. Going. To. Happen.

Grabbing the polish and a rag I start to work on the first item on my list. As I was storing provisions that were brought on board, I noticed the furniture in the main salon, sky lounge, and guest rooms all needed to be polished. As Mom always says, "If you can't see your reflection, then it's not done properly."

The main guest cabin is almost all set and only needs this final touch. Last night I had finished making the bed, scrubbed down the bathroom, fluffed the pillows and set mints out, and restocked the towels so it looks spotless to the untrained eye.

Grabbing the vase of fresh flowers off the side table, I notice the surface is already polished, my confused face looking back at me in the reflection.

What the hell?

In fact, every surface has already been wiped down. Surely someone didn't take it upon themselves to do this right? But it's not like I would have noticed. I was too busy in the storage areas to know if someone was still up and working. Maybe it was Keeran? She knew I was planning to work late and it feels like it's something she would do.

Hmmm.... interesting. No point in dwelling on it, I guess.

The funny thing is, almost everything on my list has been taken care of. It seems my secret helper worked their magic while I was in the bowels of the damn ship.

If I could kiss them, I would.

Through the radio, Damon announces that breakfast is ready, so I stop by the galley and snag a muffin, blowing a kiss at him as I leave. He's such a fun person to flirt with even though I have no romantic feelings for him. It's important that we get along with one another since the two of us will be working closely and I think we've hit it off wonderfully.

Muffin in hand, I bounce down the steps into the laundry room. Now that all the housekeeping upstairs is done, I need to get uniforms all sorted. It's my responsibility to clean and iron the crew uniforms and to make sure they get to the correct people.

When I first arrived, I placed all their motor yacht *Siren* staples on their beds, all except what we call our whites, which are our more formal uniforms that needed to be steamed. Being a crew member on a yacht is full of outfit changes, which sounds ridiculous, and it is. We all get t-shirts and tennis shoes, and the deck crew gets shorts while I get a skort—that ridiculous skirt-short combo that's popular with toddlers.

The laundry room is a place where time and the outside world cease to exist. There are no windows in here, only the low hum of the dryers and never-ending laundry. Most stews hate the laundry room and avoid it at all costs, but to me, it's the best place to think. Folding and ironing take little to no brain power, so my mind wanders, and believe me, all I can think about is Captain Pike's hands on me.

My mind replays how it felt as his large hand gripped my ass and lifted me to the counter so effortlessly it made me feel like I was weightless. Of how his hand caressed my leg as he knelt to look at my foot. Every tiny, seemingly insignificant interaction with him has me heated.

Time passes quickly and before I know it, Captain announces through the radio that the Oliviers will be arriving soon. Scooping the freshly steamed uniforms up, I drop them off with each crewmember before changing into my own.

"Hannah, Hannah, Captain." Captain Pike's deep voice rumbles through the speaker.

"Go for Hannah," I reply, looping my radio into my belt and fitting the earpiece. I give myself one last look over in the mirror, dabbing some concealer under my eyes to hide the dark circles there thanks to my long night of working.

"Am I going to get my uniform at some point?" He doesn't sound annoyed, but he doesn't sound happy either.

Fuck. I forgot his uniform.

"I'm so sorry, I'll bring it up to you now." The man seems to be in a perpetual state of grumpiness, so I must already be on his bad side. Now, this? Ugh. It's going to be a rough few weeks.

Sure enough, the captain's uniform is hanging right where I left it. With a sigh, I grab it and practically jog up the steps to the bridge hoping the faster I get it there, the less angry he'll be.

The captain's quarters on this boat are located on the bridge so the captain is never far from the control center.

A bit winded from my sprint up the steps, I knock lightly on his door and wait.

"Come in." His voice is muffled by the door, and I carefully open it, unaware of what lies beyond it.

Captain Pike is almost completely naked. Well, he's not naked, but damn do I wish he was. He's wearing a towel, tied tight across his waist leaving little to the imagination. I don't know whether to turn away or keep staring. I should turn away, right?

Looking at him leaves me in a trance. I'm completely frozen by his beauty. He's tanned all over, the skin of this toned stomach glistening from his recent shower. His chest is sculptured and lightly speckled with the chest hair that I imagine rubbing against my nipples as he thrusts into me, sending a wave of desire down my spine.

"Thanks, Hannah." He looks up at me then and I realize my eyes never left his body. Not a soul can blame me for staring either because the man in front of me is more a Greek demi-god than a man.

Holy. Shit.

"Hannah." His voice is deep and gravelly and when my gaze finally meets his, it's like all the air is sucked from the room. In an instant, he pulls me towards him in a tight embrace, the uniform I so carefully steamed crushed between us as he slips his hand around my neck and pulls my lips to his.

I'm vaguely aware of his other hand squeezing and kneading my ass, pulling my hips flush against his but my focus is on his mouth. Our lips slick together and I'm freely giving what he's taking. And that's what he's doing: taking. There's nothing gentle about this kiss. It's fierce and passionate and it almost brings me to my knees with its intensity.

His tongue teases my own and there's no holding back my moan of pleasure. At this, his hand cradling my head fists in my ponytail sending fresh desire pooling in my core. He doesn't pull, but squeezes, making goosebumps pop up on my skin.

I've never been dominated before, but this must be what it feels like. He's in complete control and that's exactly where I want him.

When my hands settle on the bare skin of his waist, he lets out a predatory groan that sets my blood boiling. He guides us backward, my back pressing against the closed door of his cabin and the feeling of being trapped by him is intoxicating. The hand grabbing my ass moves lower, his fingers inching up the hem of my formal pencil skirt.

Oh god, I want this. He's had me turned on all damn day since the moment he walked into the galley and my time daydreaming in the laundry room has had me on edge.

I *want* his touch. I *need* his touch. I *crave* his touch.

Just as his hand slides under the fabric of my underwear, the static of the radio makes us pause.

"Captain, Captain, Garrett."

Our faces are a hair's breadth away from each other and when our eyes meet, his are wide with... regret? Panic? I'm not sure.

Slowly, he removes his hand from under my skirt, leaving me feeling cold without his touch. Instead of letting me go to find his radio, he reaches up and grabs the speaker hanging from my collar, bringing it to his lips.

"Yes?" How he manages to sound normal while I can feel his sizable erection digging into my stomach, I'll never know.

"Captain, the Oliviers are walking down the dock. Looks like they are arriving early."

"Copy." Captain Pike's eyes never leave mine as he releases his hand and steps back.

I feel strange without him pressing into me, holding me, controlling me. All I can do is stare as he walks to the table beside his bed and picks up his radio.

"All crew, all crew, you're needed on the aft deck in five minutes." His voice rings out around me, the echo of his words replaying through the earpiece.

The responses of the crew sound more like the adults in a Charlie Brown movie for all I can comprehend right now. Part of me is convinced this is a fantasy, that it all happened in my head, but it didn't. His dick is hard, straining against the towel and my heart is thrumming wildly in my chest.

Wordlessly, he walks to me clutching his towel before scooping his uniform off the floor where it fell when he pulled away. He straightens and I can see his jaw clenching.

Fuck me, there's something so sexy about that subtle move.

"Thank you, Hannah." His normal gruff tone is gone, replaced with one that sounds more morose.

Does he not want me? Does he think this is a mistake?

It takes a moment for me to respond. What does he want me to say? You're welcome? Shit, I should be saying thank you. That was the hottest damn thing I've ever experienced.

Unsure of what to do, I settle for a quick nod before leaving and closing the door behind me.

I would be lying if I said my legs are steady as I climb down the steps and make my way through the boat. My knees wobble with every step and there's an obnoxious throbbing between my legs that makes it hard to focus on anything else.

The aft deck is bathed in sunlight and it's pure luck that several crew members still haven't made it. I stand next to Garrett, his tall frame towering over me. There hasn't been much time to learn about him but he's so serious. He's been kind, but his face seems stuck in a scowl.

"So," I start, trying to push back what I'm feeling by focusing on something else, "are you excited?" Unable to stand still, I reach up and fiddle with my ponytail, worried that it's ruined from our moment of passion.

"I'm just ready to get underway and off this dock." He links his hands behind his back looking more like a military man than a first officer.

Aidan saves me from this one-sided conversation as he bounds down the steps leading to the sky lounge. "Where the hell is everyone?" He casually sticks his hand down the front of his slacks adjusting his tucked white shirt as he comes to a stop next to me.

Aidan is cute in a free spirit sort of way. He's lean and tan with long chocolate-brown hair highlighted from the sun. It's just long enough to be pulled back in a small bun and it fits his whole vibe.

Garrett mutters a quick "Don't know" while I shrug at him.

Damon strolls in wearing his chef's jacket and gives me a cocky wink before squeezing between me and Aidan, making him scoot over to make room.

"I'm here!" Keeran comes jogging down the port side trying to button her top as she comes to a stop beside Aidan just as the double doors to the main salon whoosh open.

Seeing Captain Pike after that kiss makes it difficult to look away from him. My eyes are glued to his lips which moments ago were ravaging mine.

Captain stands on the other side of Garrett, his gaze sliding past me and down the row. It's like he doesn't even see me. I'm a little insulted by that, but not as much as I would be if I didn't know his reaction to my touch.

God, the way he groaned into my mouth...

Instead of standing awkwardly and forcing myself to not look at him as my mind plays the kiss on repeat, I turn and look down the dock squinting from the sunlight. Two familiar figures walk toward us and a grin breaks out of my face.

Dr. and Mr. Olivier are the classiest people I've seen in real life.

Dr. Grace Olivier is the epitome of class and at sixty-five she still exudes beauty and elegance. Growing up, I used to think of her as an angel with her graceful movements and soft voice. Her silver hair shines in the sunlight, her casual dress blows in the light breeze. She's who I hoped I looked like when I arrived yesterday before it went sideways.

Her husband, Mark Olivier, is some type of finance guru. He's nice enough, but I never got as close to him as I did with Grace. Like his wife, he looks years younger than he actually is. It's easy to see that he still works out, the fitted button-up shows that off well enough.

When they're close enough to see me, I wave enthusiastically with both hands drawing chuckles from Keeran.

"Whoa, don't I feel late to the party." Completely unfazed by how late he is, Robbie strolls through the doors with a lazy grin, pushing his floppy hair away from his face.

"That's because you are." I'm surprised it wasn't Captain's voice, but Garrett's that chastises him.

Robbie just shrugs as he takes his place, completely unbothered by Garrett's cool tone, "Nature calls." Keeran hides her mouth with her hand trying and failing to stifle her chuckles.

Damn, she's got it bad.

Damon mumbles under his breath, "Get your game faces on wankers," as Captain turns and greets our guests.

Guests? Owners? Who even knows at this point?

Captain Pike welcomes them aboard and introduces the rest of the crew to them going down the line. Everyone is all smiles and politely waves when it's their turn. Once introductions are made Captain fills them in on the travel plans before leaving them to my care.

The moment Captain leaves for the bridge, Dr. Olivier throws her arms around me in a big hug. "Hannah, it's so good to see you. I'm so glad you decided to come back to us, we love having you here."

"I love being here," I reply, hugging her back.

Grace pulls back and Mark steps in to give me a quick side hug. "Good to see you, kid."

"I have everything ready for you," I say, sliding into the stewardess role and motioning them into the main salon. "Everything is set up just like you like it. The chef will have lunch whenever you're ready and can go over the menu with you if you would like."

"Oh, that sounds wonderful. You've done such a good job." Her eyes dart around the room, and Grace pats my shoulder as we reach the steps that lead down to the guest cabins.

"Can I get you anything?" I'm proud of the work I've put in but I always feel like there's more I should be doing.

"I'd like a glass of gin and tonic. Grace?" Mark caresses her back gently as he leads her to their room.

"Oh, I think I'd like a white wine spritzer. Thank you."

I leave them to get settled and head to the bar to make their drinks. Aidan and Robbie carry the luggage onto the aft deck, both huffing and puffing at the heavy suitcases as Keeran watches them, bowing over with laughter that makes me chuckle.

This is going to be a good few weeks, I can feel it.

Chapter Six

Anson

This week on the boat with Hannah has been hell.

Why did I have to lose control like that? It was a stupid fucking mistake and now I have to live with the consequences.

Meaning my dick is constantly hard at the sight of her.

Nothing, not the crystal blue waves, running the boat, or the threat of severe weather can take my mind off of her.

Since that first morning, Hannah has been up bright and early and always brings me a steaming mug of coffee. She doesn't say anything other than good morning and aside from radio communication, she's been silent.

And it's killing me.

Everything about her is killing me. The way she smiles at Damon, her playfulness with Keeran, and I've caught her laughing and chatting with Aidan in the crew mess. Jealousy threatens to overtake me and I'm not one to get jealous.

What is it about this girl?

One fucking moment of weakness and a lifetime of torture. At least that's what it feels like after learning how she tastes and knowing it can never happen again.

I watch while she packs a supply bag for the Oliviers with anything they could need while away. We anchored outside of Nassau last night and today they head ashore with Aidan, who Garrett appointed for Bosun. It's a solid choice and who I would have gone with.

Her eyebrows furrow as she checks and double-checks the items in the bag leaving little wrinkles on her brow. It's so fucking cute that I want to kiss those little wrinkles one by one until they fade away.

"Everything okay there, love?" Damon's voice is teasing and full of amusement. The kind I wish I had with her.

She's so caught up in her task that I can see the moment she registers that someone's talking to her. Those blue eyes shoot up in confusion. "Huh?"

Damon chuckles as he bends to rummage through the cabinets. "You looked like you were having a hard time. Would you like some help, beautiful?"

"Um, I think I have it now. Thanks, cheffy." She puckers those lips that I can't forget the feel of at him and makes a smooching noise. "You know I love ya."

Jealousy flows through me at their exchange, and I can't take it anymore. I finish scrubbing my coffee mug in the sink and set it down to dry too hard to go unnoticed. The mug clinks loudly against the stainless steel counter and their eyes shoot to me.

So much for my control.

"You alright, Captain?" Damon's voice is the last thing I want to hear right now. Part of me wants to wrap my hands around his neck and squeeze, but it's not his fault. He can talk to her freely. He can flirt and tease her without anyone thinking twice. He gets to have a relationship with her while I'm stuck with memories of her touch.

Finishing drying my hands with a paper towel, I nod. "An accident."

YES, CAPTAIN

Hannah's gaze catches mine and we stare at each other for a moment. The last time our eyes met was in my room with her in my arms. Her breath on my skin.

Again, her eyebrows furrow, and this time her face isn't one of concentration, but of concern. Maybe she's feeling the same things I am.

I guess I'll never know.

I can feel her eyes on my back as I walk past her and up the stairs to the bridge. Every fiber of my being wants to turn and look at her beautiful face, but I force myself not to.

When I reach the top of the steps, Garrett's sitting in the bridge staring over the glistening water. It's easy to see how dedicated he is to his job. The man is constantly working, possibly even more than I do.

Silently, I sit in the booth that backs against my cabin wall and pull out the course navigations. The Oliviers made specific requests and I've got to finalize our course.

After several minutes of the two of us working in silence, Hannah's voice breaks over the radio. "Garrett, the Oliviers are ready for departure." Since Aidan is traveling with them, Garrett will be the one driving the tender to drop them off.

"Copy." With a sigh, Garrett pushes himself out of the chair and leaves.

My mind settles into the routine and order of maps, mentally outlining our route when the faint sound of steps coming up the stairs pulls my focus.

Hannah comes to a stop in front of me and the breath is knocked from my lungs. The sun is shining through the bay of windows backlighting the gorgeous woman in front of me.

Her eyes are wide and nervously dart around the room before settling on me.

"Can I talk to you?" Her fists clench at her sides, making my cock hard.

"Sure," I say, closing the work in front of me and giving her all my attention.

She glances around the room while biting her lip. "Not here," she whispers.

So not a work-related conversation then.

Shivers of anticipation travel down my spine. We've both been dodging each other since that mistake, and I had hoped it wouldn't be brought up again.

Hell, even I know that's a damned lie. Every night I've gone to sleep with the feel of her lips in my mind and my hand on my cock.

There aren't many places where two people can be alone on this boat, let alone one where no one would see us going there. "My cabin okay?" She nods and I gesture to the door to my right. "After you."

Quietly the door clicks closed behind me. Hannah has her back to me, her shoulders heaving with her breathing. Suddenly she whirls around, her face a mask of hidden fury. "What the hell is wrong with you?" Her voice is a demanding whisper, aware that there are many others on board who could overhear us. "I don't know who you think you are, but you *cannot* just kiss me like that and then ignore me." She points her finger toward me as she talks, making me want to tie those hands behind her back. "You're such a—"

Reaching behind me, I flip the lock on the door and walk toward her.

"What are you doing?" she whispers, breathless.

With each step forward, Hannah steps back until her back thumps the closed bathroom door. Her chest is heaving, that vein in her neck pounding in time with her heartbeat. Slowly, I lift my hand to caress her throat, my large hand resting on both sides of her slender neck. She shudders at the connection but doesn't try to break the contact.

"Hannah," I growl with a crooked grin. "I'm going to teach you a fucking lesson." Every ounce of resolve is demolished the moment she gasps as my lips meet hers. I've been dreaming of her lips against mine all fucking week and that pales in comparison to the real thing.

"Do you know what you're doing to me, Hannah? Do you know how much I want you?" My lips flutter against her jaw as I lightly apply pressure to her neck. The moan she releases is the best fucking sound I've ever heard. "Oh, Hannah. Do you like that? Do you want me to teach you a lesson?" Her pulse is wild now, thrumming against my palm, making me want to see how fast I can get it.

Her hips grind against mine and there's no stopping the groan she drags from me. "Yes, Captain. I want that. Teach me." Between her ragged breaths, her voice is deep and sultry.

It's the answer to all my desires.

"Baby, you have no idea the things I'm going to do to you."

"Are you all talk or are you going to follow through?" Her chin juts defiantly at me in a challenge. Oh, this girl is begging for a spanking but now's not the time.

"Hands above your head, and don't drop them." Hannah's lust-filled gaze meets mine as she licks her lips but doesn't respond. "Do you understand, Hannah?" She's a brat that needs taming, but I don't have the patience for that now.

There's not enough time for me to make her beg properly.

Those blue eyes shine with defiance as she slowly raises her arms over her head, granting me permission. "Do your worst, Captain."

Fuck. Me.

"Oh, Hannah," I chastise, stepping back from her and raking my eyes down her stunning body. "You have no idea."

With the way she's been killing me this week, I want to make her feel my torment and I know just what to do.

Stalking forward, my hands settle around her hips and she can't help but fidget. She rubs her thighs together, her weight shifting between them.

She's a needy one.

My thumbs hook in the elastic waistband of her skirt and underwear, slowly dragging both down deliberately, painstakingly slow. Her breathing picks up as I kneel before her, her hot cunt inches away from my mouth.

I've waited so damn long for this.

In one swift movement, I throw her right leg over my shoulder and run my index finger through her wet folds. Hannah's head thumps against the door behind her as I watch her face, see her lips part, and hear the soft moan escape them.

"You're so wet, baby. So fucking wet for me. Have you been wanting me on my knees in front of you, baby?" My finger strokes against her clit and she bites her lip with a groan. "So beautiful." I groan as I explore her with slow, deliberate movements meant to drive her mad, and they do. Her hips rock into my touch, trying to get my fingers where she wants them, but it's no use.

I'm the one in control now.

"Oh my god," she moans as I lightly rub against her clit, barely giving her what she wants. It's here when she finally breaks. Those arms, once hanging above her head, fall to her sides as she loses herself in sensations. Immediately I withdraw my hand, clicking my tongue in disapproval.

"What the fuck are you doing?" She's breathless and frustrated and so fucking beautiful.

"Oh Hannah," I sigh, looking up into her lust-filled eyes. "Why'd you have to go and do that?" Her eyes go wide when she realizes her mistake and quickly raises her hands back over her head, but it's too late now.

Slowly I lower her leg back to the floor and stand, deliberately tugging her shirt up in the process.

Let's see how she responds to nipple stimulation.

The top slides over her head and I make quick work of her bra, tossing it to the side. Her arms stay glued above her head but I can see that she's struggling, her muscles twitching with the effort to keep them elevated.

I can remedy that.

Removing my belt with a snap, I grab her small wrists, making make-shift handcuffs before latching the leather band over the towel hook on the back of the door. Now she's completely at my disposal.

I want to feel her skin, her body, against mine.

Gripping the back of my shirt, I pull it over my head and toss it to the side. I can feel Hannah's eyes on me as she swallows hard. "Like what you see, baby?"

The buckle of my belt rattles against the door as she tries to move her hands. "I'd like it better if you didn't take so damn long." The sight of her naked, tied up, and ready for me will forever be seared into my memory.

"Your wish is my command." My mouth finds her neck and she arches into me, her beautiful breast rubbing against my chest. She lets out a long groan, her body writhing against mine. Dipping my head lower I lick the tight bud of her nipple and she sucks in a sharp breath.

"That's it, baby. Let me hear you." My mouth toys with one nipple while my hand caresses the other. She struggles against her bindings the more I nip and suckle, driving her wild. My palm glides down her chest, over her hip, and slips back between her thighs. "So fucking wet," I praise.

I can't take it anymore. I need to know what she tastes like. Need to know the sounds she makes when my lips wrap around that little bud between her legs.

She doesn't disappoint.

"Fuck," she gasps as my mouth finds her center. Her taste on my tongue is heaven. Swirling my tongue through her wet folds, hearing her mewling whimpers, her hips bucking against me is everything I've wanted since I watched her on the dock. My hands squeeze her ass, rocking her against my face, but it's not enough. I need more.

"Put your legs over my shoulders, baby. I've got you." She doesn't hesitate. My shoulders support her weight as I devour every seductive inch of her perfect pussy until her legs begin to shake, her back arching away from the door.

She's under my complete control and it's fucking beautiful.

Hannah comes, her thighs clamping around my head, her body spasming as I continue to lick her. When her body goes limp, I lower her legs and remove my pants.

My cock is hard and slick with precum. Hannah's eyes, heavy with lust, watch as I step toward her, lifting her leg to lock around my hips.

"Wait." We're face to face now, our bodies flush from chest to hips. "What's your name? I need to know the first name of the man I'm fucking." She smiles at me softly, nervously and I can't help but smile back.

"Anson," I say. "My name is Anson."

Her blue eyes lock with mine. "Fuck me, Anson."

The tip of my cock slides through her folds, teasing. I take my time, the palm of my hand resting against her neck, applying light pressure. "This pussy is mine," I hiss, slamming into her in one smooth motion.

Her pussy flutters around my cock, her muscles squeezing and releasing in sweet agony. Her face is the picture of pure ecstasy, her luscious lips parted as she gasps.

"You're so fucking beautiful. Look at you taking my cock like a good fucking girl." Her eyes roll into her head with each thrust. Our bodies are slick with sweat, the door at her back rattling with each movement.

"Anson," she moans, her pussy gripping my cock in a vise. "I'm going to—" Her body explodes in an earth-rattling orgasm. She cries out, my name on her lips as she climaxes, and I drown out her cries with my mouth. I kiss her through her orgasm dampening her cries as I continue to thrust into her tight pussy until I can hold out no longer. With one final thrust, my cock jerks and I shudder my release.

SIERRA SHIPLEY

There's no turning back now.

Chapter Seven

Hannah

Well, this is not what I had expected to happen, but I sure as shit am not going to complain about it.

He's been driving me crazy all week. Not once did he look at me after that kiss. Not once did he seek me out. And damn it, I wanted him to.

And it pissed me off.

You can't kiss a girl like that and give her the cold shoulder, then brood about it to the point where you're mad at everyone. People were starting to notice it too. Once the Oliviers were off the boat, I figured I'd take the chance and give him a piece of my mind.

I got more than I bargained for.

More like the only two orgasms I've ever had with a partner, more.

My body is still shaking with aftershocks, Anson buried deep inside me. His large hand around my throat is more like a caress than a threat, the gentle squeeze enough to drive me wild.

Anson groans into my neck before pressing his forehead against mine. "What are you doing to me?" He asks, his voice is raw and full of awe.

I chuckle, my hands straining against the door. "I can say the same thing."

He slowly pulls himself from me and immediately I feel lonely without his touch. His hands trail up my torso to my arms above my head as he ever so gently removes the belt and rubs the tension from my muscles. "You did so well, baby."

"I can't take all the credit. I didn't give myself two toe-curling orgasms. That was all you." Shit, I didn't mean to say that. All these feel-good endorphins flooding my system have also loosened my damn lips.

He chuckles and brings my wrists to his mouth kissing them lightly. "I'll aim for three next time."

This man is a dream come true.

"There's going to be a next time?" The thought of him commanding my body over and over again has new waves of pleasure snaking down my spine. The man has said more words to me in the past twenty minutes than he did all week and now he wants there to be a next time.

Do I want there to be a next time? Absolutely. There's only the minor problem that he's my boss and we're stuck together on a boat with very little privacy, but the thought of getting caught in a compromising position kind of turns me on.

Okay, not kind of, but a lot.

"That all depends on you, Hannah." His eyes bore into mine as he continues. "I've tried to stay away from you, but I lose control when it comes to you. I need to have you Hannah, but you say the word and it won't happen again. You call the shots."

I answer without hesitating. "Yes, Captain," I say with a smile. "There will be a next time." Anson pulls me close and kisses me hard, leaving me breathless.

By the time I'm dressed and ready to leave, my feet don't want to move. I don't want to leave this bubble.

Instead of sneaking through the bridge and the galley below, I step out of the side door and onto the top deck of the ship. Garrett should be back any minute and I don't want to risk running into him or seeing Damon in the galley.

I can hear Robbie and Keeran as they work on scrubbing the boat down, their voices playful and teasing. Nothing's happened between them yet, but I guarantee something will happen before we leave the boat. The two of them are always cuddling in the crew mess during dinner or downtime.

The sun feels warm on my skin, and I let it wash over me. It's not often that I get to enjoy the sunshine with all the interior work I have to do. Breathing a deep sigh, I make my way through the boat and back inside to work.

I am *so* looking forward to next time.

• • • •

"OH, HANNAH?" DR. OLIVIER places her hand on my arm as I pour her a glass of orange juice the next morning. "I wanted to tell you that Keith will be on board with us next week. We'll pick him up tomorrow. Isn't that lovely?"

Lovely? For whom? Keith is an asshat, and I can't stand him.

Gritting my teeth, I give a polite smile and try my best to not sound annoyed. "How nice. I'll make sure the guest room is all set for him."

Keith would visit his grandparents every summer which meant that a lot of the time, I was forced to play with him. He's older than me and always tried to force me to play games I didn't want to play. What's worse is that when we got older, he thought he was entitled to me, entitled to everything.

I hate him.

He pretends to be a good person, but he's an arrogant asshole. He learned quickly that I won't put up with his shit. Pretty sure a fist to his testicles, when I was sixteen, cleared that right up.

But him being on board? I'm not sure how it's going to go.

When you're on a yacht working, you're expected to put up with any type of inappropriate comments or dickish behavior from a guest. Many times, I've had to hold my tongue and grin and bear it just to keep my job. I have this feeling that Keith will take advantage of that.

Only now he'll have the entire crew to boss around and follow his every whim.

Anson, Captain Pike, said they were expecting to have some guests, I just didn't think it would be him.

Last summer, Mark's sister and her husband joined them for a week, and they were such nice people.

Keith isn't. Not even close.

When I climb into bed after sprucing up the guest room for Keith, I unload on Keeran.

"I'll keep my eye on him. One wrong move and I'll go straight to Captain." She leans down the ledge of our bunk bed, her long hair dangling. "I've got your back."

"Thanks," I sigh, squeezing Henry closer to my chest hoping to alleviate the ball of stress that's settled there. "I don't think he'll do anything, but still. I hate the guy."

"Well, get some sleep tonight. Dream about punching his balls." We both giggle before saying goodnight.

The thought of telling Keeran about what happened between the captain and me has crossed my mind, but I stay silent. There's something thrilling and dangerous about sneaking around and I love it.

Not to mention the small issue that we'd both be fired if anyone found out.

It doesn't take long before Keeran's soft snore drifts through the cabin. I know it's late, but sleep doesn't come. Frustrated, I fling the covers over my legs and quietly leave the room.

I head to the bow of the boat hoping some fresh air will do the trick.

Waves lap at the sides, the gentle sloshing sounds soothing my nerves. It's so quiet out here. Peaceful. I don't know how long I've been standing here looking out across the dark sea illuminated by the moon and twinkling stars, but soft footsteps coming towards me have me turning.

Anson walks towards me wearing shorts and a soft V-neck. "Looks like I wasn't the only one who couldn't sleep tonight." His gray-speckled blond hair looks rough with sleep, and it makes him that much more handsome.

"How did you know I was here?" I ask, trying to keep my voice from wavering. He smiles and points up the bridge.

"It wasn't hard to spot you." He stops beside me, our shoulders brushing as he leans against the railing. "What's on your mind?"

Is this what I signed up for? Is this what *he* signed up for? Something about this question makes me feel like we're entering relationship territory and I'm not sure if that's what either of us wants. To me, the chemistry between us is explosive and can't be denied, but does that automatically mean that we're *together,* together?

When I don't respond, he nudges me with his shoulder. "I don't mean to pry, it just seemed like you were working through something."

"It's not that, I just—," I turn to face him, "I'm not sure what *this* is." I gesture between the two of us. "I can't figure out if you're being nice or if you're interested in me." He blinks slowly at me, taking me in.

"Hannah, I think it's pretty clear that I'm interested in you." His blue eyes are soft as he looks at me, his voice gentle.

"For sex, obviously, but I meant like me as a person. Are we just having sex or what?" I'm not doing a good job at all this. We've only had sex once with the promise of more, but what lies beyond that?

Anson straightens to face me. "Not just sex." His voice is deep and his blue eyes lock onto mine. "There's something about you that draws me to you. I've never felt that before, and believe me, I tried to fight it. You're something special, Hannah, and I'd very much like to get to know you." My mouth hangs open in surprise because holy shit I was not expecting that. He chuckles and shrugs his shoulders. "And the sex is pretty fucking awesome."

Laughing, I smack at his arm. "Oh my god, keep your voice down," I hiss, worried someone will overhear us.

His smile is breathtaking. "We're the only two up. I sent Robbie to bed an hour ago since I couldn't sleep. No use in having two people up to do anchor watch."

"So," I whisper, stepping closer, "how long do we have before anyone else is up?" His eyes flash with recognition as he takes in my meaning.

He leans in close, barely brushing my lips with his. "Hours." My insides melt as a flood of anticipation courses through my body.

"Then what are we waiting for?" Wrapping my arms around his shoulders, I kiss him. He doesn't hesitate in taking control, his tongue dipping into my mouth to stroke against mine. His arms band around my waist and suddenly my feet are off the teak as he holds me closer to him. I lose all sense of time and place as he devours me, consuming me whole.

Fuck, I've never been kissed like this.

When he sets me back down on the solid floor of the deck, we're both breathless. "Meet me in my room in five minutes." He waits for me to nod before turning and heading back up to the bridge.

Okay, so I'm doing this. I'm *really* doing this. Being with Anson is more than just sex and my heart flutters nervously at the thought. This could be more than the run-of-the-mill boat-mance. This could turn into a full-blown relationship.

The thought is both nerve-wracking and exciting.

The bridge is dark and empty when I get there, the only lights coming from the many displays and panels of the control center. Anson's door is closed and for a moment I'm not sure what to do. Part of me feels like we're so far past knocking at this point, and he *is* expecting me. Sucking in a deep breath, I push the door open.

Anson sits on his bed, completely naked, his large cock jutting straight into the air. "Lock the door." Holy shit, he's my dream man. "Take your clothes off, baby." He's so controlling and demanding. It makes me wet.

Slowly I peel my sleep shirt over my head, taking my time to tease him as much as possible, my fingers toying with my nipples as he watches. He bites his lips when my shorts glide down my long legs, pooling on the floor beneath me leaving me completely bare. "Better?"

"Oh, baby, you have no idea what I have planned for you and that smart mouth." If I could be set on fire from words alone, I think that would've done it.

I reach for him, stepping closer until I'm standing over him, but he pulls back, grabbing my hands in his.

"Have you ever been spanked, Hannah?" My head jerks back at his question. Is he...? Does he want to spank me?

"Um," I swallow, "when I was a kid, sometimes. Not for a long time though." The image of me draped over his lap, his large hand smacking against my ass has me turned the fuck on.

"Can I spank you, Hannah?" He releases my hands dropping his to glide up my thighs and grip the globes of my ass as his mouth settles over my nipple and sucks. I inhale a ragged breath, my hands twisting in his hair.

"Yes," I breathe. "Spank me, Captain."

His growl reverberates against my nipple, adding a new sensation with the sucking and I moan.

"I fucking love it when you call me captain. Now get on my lap, I want to see that perfect ass in the air." He releases me and I do as I'm told and lay across his strong thighs. "Everyone might be asleep, but we still have to be quiet. If it gets to be too much, I need you to tell me. Understand?"

"Yes." A sharp slap on my left ass cheek has me covering my mouth with a yelp.

"Yes, what?"

"Yes, Captain."

"Good girl," he praises, voice rough and strained. "This is for that mouth of yours, baby." Another slap stings across my cheeks that's quickly followed by the soothing touch of his hand. Again, his hand connects with my skin, this time lower and I feel his palm press against my pussy. Again and again, he spanks me, followed quickly by a soothing touch until I'm writhing with need. I can feel the slickness between my legs and when he sinks a finger into me, I moan into the sheets I've fisted over my mouth to stifle my moans of pleasure.

"Fuck, you're perfect, aren't you. This pussy likes to be commanded, doesn't it baby? It likes what I'm doing to you."

I can only moan my response as he sinks another finger into me, pushing in and out of my wet pussy.

"Sit up and ride my dick, baby. Let me feel that hot cunt of yours squeeze around me."

He doesn't have to tell me twice. I scramble off his lap and quickly straddle his hips, lining him up with my soaked entrance and gliding down making us both moan as I take him deep.

"That's it, baby. Fuck me." Rising up on my knees, I sink back down onto him. He feels so good inside me, making me lose my mind. His hands grip my ass, pulling me deeper down onto him. "You're so fucking beautiful, riding my cock like a goddess." He continues to whisper into my ear, ratcheting up my pleasure with every dirty word, every moan.

I'm completely lost to the world, the only thing that matters at this moment is his body and mine, the two of us losing ourselves in each other.

Higher and higher the pleasure builds until I'm whimpering with the need for release. His hand reaches between our two bodies fondling my clit at the same time as his mouth latches around my nipple and I come with a muffled scream. Head thrown back, my body bows against him, losing all control. I come so hard I can barely breathe, my vision turning spotty around the edges.

Anson pulls me closer to him, burying himself deep one last time before he joins me.

Yeah, this is about to get *so* complicated.

Chapter Eight

Anson

Hannah is so fucking perfect.

I find myself daydreaming of her as I stand on the aft deck waiting for our new arrival.

Aidan and his crew have done well keeping the boat in top shape. Keeran and Aidan lower the jet skis to the water for the Oliviers who have been ideal guests; pleasant and polite.

Across the water, I can see Garrett in the tender escorting the grandson on board.

Hannah's laughing voice drifts down from the sky lounge deck where Mr. Olivier is working on his laptop. Absently, I wonder if her ass is sore and I have to admit the thought makes me smile.

God, how fucking wet she was for me.

I managed to follow through on the promise I made to her, wringing two more orgasms from her before we lay in my bed cuddled together. She spoke about her life growing up and told cherished stories about her father. She lights up when she talks about her travels and all the places she wants to visit and I listened happily, soaking up everything she has to offer.

Never have I felt anything this intense. The need to touch her, see her, taste her is almost overwhelming.

Garrett glides the tender to the *Siren*, and Robbie quickly anchors the small vessel, tying the lines off swiftly and efficiently.

The man that steps from the boat is the picture of arrogance. He's wearing salmon-colored shorts and a white polo shirt which accentuates the orange tone of fake tanner on his skin. His teeth are overly white making me think they forgot about him while getting his teeth whitened. His head is covered in a mop of curls quickly turning poofy from the humidity.

"Hey man, thanks for the ride." He offers his hand to me in greeting. "Keith. And you are?"

Grasping his hand in a firm shake, I say, "Captain Pike." There's something about him that sets me on edge. Maybe it's the cocky set of his jaw.

"Oh, nice." His eyes glance past my shoulder and a predatory smile crosses his lips. "Hannah." The way he sighs her name has me wanting to punch those over-white teeth from his mouth.

"Keith. Can I get you anything?" She stands at the bottom of the steps of the swim platform, her arms crossed. The smile on her face is polite but doesn't reach her eyes, making me pause. This isn't like her.

"A hug would be nice." It's official, I hate this guy.

Hannah slowly steps forward, her arms unwinding to rest by her side but not wrapping around him. Instead, she stands stock still as he pulls her to him.

The sight of her in his arms has me filled with rage. I want to pull her from his arms and wrap her in mine.

He murmurs something in her ear too soft for me to hear and Hannah pulls back with a sudden jerk. "I would be happy to get you *anything else* you might need." It doesn't go unnoticed that her tone is firm and friendly but with a commanding air.

Keith chuckles, looking down and shaking his head. "You know, sex on the beach sounds pretty good right now."

What the fuck?

My fists clench at my sides as Hannah nods and sprints up the stairs to the aft deck to make his drink.

I'm going to have to keep an eye on this guy.

He's been on the boat for three hours and he's already running Hannah ragged. He orders drink after drink to be brought to him, has her unpacking his bags, and constantly does things that frustrates her. She grins politely, but the set of her jaw says anything but.

Throughout the dinner service, I work side by side with Hannah. With one more person on the boat, more hands are needed for service and there's no way in hell I'm going to let anyone else do it. There's a sense that this slimy Keith fucker has something up his sleeves and I'm banking on the fact that he won't do it in front of me.

Damon is cooking a six-course tasting menu, courtesy of the prick. The minute he shook the chef's hand he practically demanded it. Damon has been stressed out all day preparing the menu and he's insisting on total silence as he plates.

My arm twitches with the need to wrap around Hannah as we wait for Damon to finish plating this course. She's been fidgeting since this morning and right now, she's bouncing on the balls of her feet, unable to stand still. I'm surprised Damon hasn't snapped at her yet.

There's an underlying history between Hannah and Keith and I want to know more. Is he an ex? Does he know what she sounds like as she comes?

Jealousy is quickly becoming my constant companion and I have to get a hold of myself. She clearly doesn't like him and is only doing her job without doing something to get her fired.

Damon finishes plating the sea bass with a flourish. "They're good to go." Hannah grabs two plates and I grab the remaining one and follow after her.

The evening breeze is pleasant as the Oliviers insist on sitting at the table on the aft deck. Hanna decorated the area with strings of twinkle lights with Aidan's help to hang them during a rare moment of downtime from Keith's orders.

The double doors open, and we step up to the tables, Hannah serving Grace and Mark while I set my plate in front of Keith. She claps her hands lightly, speaking only to Grace and Mark, her smile tight but polite. "The third course this evening is grilled sea bass on a bed of asparagus and mashed potatoes." They smile at her in thanks, and we politely leave them for their meal.

"Are you alright?" I whisper as we walk side by side back to the galley, the automatic doors shutting behind us.

Her voice is soft but tense. "I'm fine."

Call me crazy but I've been around enough women to know the words *I'm fine* mean anything but. I want to ask her about it and get down to the bottom of whatever is going on right now, but I can't.

Very carefully I brush my hand against hers. To any outsider, it might look like an accidental graze, but we know better. "Come see me tonight."

Her eyes glance over to mine, locking for a split second before she shakes her head.

Hannah completely ignores me the rest of the night. We serve the final three courses together without a word uttered between us. Silently, she places dishes next to me on the counter while I scrub what I can as Damon cleans down the stove, getting ready to head down for the night.

There's obviously something going on with her and the fact that she doesn't want to see me about it hurts. I thought I had been clear the other night when I said I wanted to know her, but maybe we aren't on the same page.

Once the dishes are finished, I do a quick walk-through of the boat, expecting the crew to be the only people awake, but I'm wrong. Keith is settled in the hot tub, beer in hand. He holds his drink up to me in greeting. "Oh, hey captain! Didn't expect to see you this evening."

I'm sure he didn't.

"Keith," I offer a polite nod as I pass by but he stops me.

"What's it like being a captain? I always thought of it as a waste, but I don't know." He gestures to the open sea around him, "This is pretty fucking awesome."

Gritting my teeth, I suck in a calming breath. "It's an adventure. Nothing but the waves and blue sky. Not a bad way to live in my opinion."

Keith scoffs. "Who fucking cares about adventure? It's the finer things in life I'm talking about. Hot tubs, servants who wait on me hand and foot, private chefs who do what I tell them to." He leans back further into the bubbling water, sighing. "I might have to convince my grandparents to let me stay."

Servants? Who the hell does he think he is? He just told me everything I needed to know about him. Now I understand why Hannah reacted the way she did.

"Well, you have a good night," I tell him tightly, before heading to the bridge. I don't want anyone to have to wait on this prick by themselves.

Robbie sits in one of the chairs on anchor watch, filling out the log on his lap. "Hey, Captain."

"Who's on lates tonight?" Each night the deck crew takes turns for anchor watch with the late shift starting around two in the morning. They monitor the anchor position, log hourly wind speeds, and scrub down the deck. Robbie finishes jotting down the anchor position before looking over at me.

"Um, I'm pretty sure it's Keeran." He slides his phone out of his pocket and shows it to me. Garrett sends them the schedule for the week, and sure enough, Keeran's name is slotted for tonight.

Crossing my arms I think, my hand sliding over my graying stubble. There's no telling how late Keith is going to be up, and I don't want either of my female crew members around him. "Keep an eye on the grandson. If he's still awake by the time Keeran's on deck, wake me up." His brown eyes widen a bit before he nods. "And help Hannah. She seems stressed," I add, doing my best to sound detached.

"Sure thing." My only answer is to slap a hand on his shoulder in thanks before trying to get some sleep.

• • • •

HANNAH STILL HASN'T left my mind by the time two o'clock rolls around. I can't stand the thought of Hannah being awake and having to take care of Keith by herself. The nagging thought has me crawling out of my bed, the need to see her overwhelming. If Keith is still around the boat I have to see for myself.

In case I get caught, I slide on my *Siren* t-shirt and shorts before leaving my cabin. I'll use the excuse of checking the boat if someone is awake and spots me. Quietly opening my door, I peek around the bridge with no one in sight.

Like a thief in the night, I sneak around the boat, going unnoticed. I make it into the galley before I hear voices and freeze.

Keeran and Robbie are in the main salon and from the sounds of it, they're *comfortable* with one another. Keeran laughs at something Robbie says, both of their voices too low for me to make out their conversation. All I need is one moment to slip into the hallway and down the stairs to the crew quarters.

It doesn't take long before I find my opening. The whoosh of the aft deck doors opening and the gusts of wind signal that they have stepped outside. It takes me less than a second to clear the hallway and go down to the crew area.

Hannah's room which she shares with Keeran is the first room on the left. Down the hall, someone snores loudly which is easily heard through the closed door. Not bothering to knock, I slide quietly into Hannah's room.

Feeling confident that Keeran is otherwise occupied, I slide off my shirt and shorts adding to the piles of clothing littering the floor before crawling into bed behind Hannah. I know she said she didn't want to see me tonight, but I can't shake the feeling that she needs me.

Hannah stiffens, her breathing no longer smooth and even. "It's me," I whisper, pulling her comforter over my exposed skin.

"Anson?" Her voice is thick with sleep and utterly adorable. "Why are you in my bed?" Even as she asks the question, her body scootches back against mine.

Do I tell her the truth?

"Well," I admit, "I thought you could use someone to talk to."

"And sneaking into my bed was your plan?"

"Was it a bad plan?" I ask. "You didn't want to come to my room, so I came to you. Do you want me to go?" She sighs as she settles her head back on her pillow.

"No, I don't want you to go." *Thank God for that.*

My arm slides against her stomach, pulling her closer to me. I wouldn't say that I've been much of a cuddler in the past, but with Hannah, there's this unshakeable need to be near her.

"You want to talk about it?" She's quiet for a moment, taking her time to think.

"I really hate him." Her words are full of disdain, and it doesn't take a genius to understand that she's talking about Keith. "He's always been an asshole, but he was on another level today."

My teeth grind together as I fight to keep a level head. "What did he say to you?" I'm telling myself that I'll be able to keep my cool, but if he said anything to hurt her, I don't know what I'll do.

"Nothing he hasn't said before," she admits. "I can deal with him; I just don't like having to. Besides," she chuckles, "I can always punch him in the balls again."

"Were you two... together?" My throat wants to swallow the words, but I have to know.

Hannah scoffs, "Fuck, no. I grew up at the Oliviers' house, and during the summers, Keith would come and visit his grandparents, so we were often forced to hang out together. When he got old enough, he... became interested in me. So, I punched him in the balls. It seemed to do the trick. Nothing helps his entitled attitude though." I feel myself start to relax at her admission.

"But he did try something today, didn't he?" Hannah's hand finds mine and she links our fingers together. She turns to face me, our linked hands nestled between our chests.

She takes a deep breath, "He always tries something." In a moment that I'll never forget, Hannah brings my hand up to her lips, kissing it sweetly. The gesture is so tender that I feel my chest tighten with emotion. "Can we talk about something else, please? "

"We can talk about whatever you want, baby." Leaning down, I plant a quick kiss on her forehead, taking a moment to breathe in the scent of her hair.

For a while, we talk comfortably in the dark quiet of her room. The more I learn about her, the more my chest fills with an emotion I've never felt before, something that's growing quickly.

"What got you into yachting?" Her voice is barely a whisper, rough and worn out from all our talking.

"Adventure," I reply without thinking. "I grew up in California, believe it or not, most of my time was spent surfing. When the opportunity arose to work on a boat, I took it and never looked back."

"Hmm," she hums. "We're a lot more alike than I thought."

"Tell me." I'll take any crumb she offers me as long as I get to keep holding her in my arms.

"There's not much to tell. I went to college and got my degree in business, but it felt... wrong," she admits. "I wanted more out of life: I wanted adventure." Her eyes meet mine, a soft smile on her face.

This girl is so much more than I could have ever imagined. We fit perfectly together, and I can see it all so clearly, how our life would be together.

But can it work? I'm thirty-eight years old, finally reaching my goal to own my own boat. She's a twenty-three-year-old stewardess just starting out in life. We both want adventure, but am I the kind of adventure she wants?

Cupping her face, my lips brush against hers. She lets out a delicious moan and leans into the kiss, deepening it. This kiss acts as a balm to my suddenly raw emotions, and she blocks out all doubt. Her long, dark hair cocoons us as she leans up on her elbows, pressing me further into the mattress. Gently, I pull back, willing those blue eyes of hers to meet mine.

"Hannah?" Her eyes are blazing with heat, but this isn't why I came here tonight. I wasn't looking for sex when I snuck out of my room to find her. I simply wanted to be with her. "Not tonight," I say as gently as I can. "I only want to hold you."

She sighs and leans down for one more kiss before settling back against me. "Goodnight, Anson. Thank you for being here for me."

I'll always want to be here for her. I'll always want to hold her.

"Goodnight, Hannah."

Chapter Nine

Hannah

My bed is toasty warm. And crowded.

Anson has his arms wrapped around my waist, pulling me against his chest. For a moment, I revel in the calm strength, and security he offers. A heavy sigh leaves my lips, my hips wiggling backward to press against him. His breaths are heavy and even, letting me know he's still sleeping, but his hands reflexively twitch in response.

Thoughts flicker through my head, not all of them innocent. If someone had told me last week that the captain that barked at me during our first meeting would be holding me close to him while he slept, I would've rolled my eyes and scoffed. But last week seems so far away. Now I know the man holding me is attentive, caring, and fucking perfect in bed.

I don't have all that much experience when it comes to sex, but I know that the chemistry between us isn't something you walk away from. We have one week left together and then all of this ends, both of us going our separate ways, but I don't want to, and I know it's all in my head. He's older than me and already knows what he wants out of life. Me? I'm a glorified maid whose only dream in life is to travel the world. There's no place for me in his life.

Not that we've talked about it.

The more time we spend together the more I learn about what goes on behind those gorgeous eyes. He's stirring up feelings inside my chest that I've never had before and the thought of leaving him brings tears to my eyes. Feeling like a stupid child, I brush the tears angrily off my cheeks.

Warm lips press against my neck as Anson sighs and nuzzles closer to me, a deep hum reverberating in his chest. "Hannah?"

Embarrassment colors my cheeks as I suck in a large breath, willing my voice to sound somewhat normal. "I didn't mean to wake you. Go back to sleep."

"Like I could with your ass grinding against me," he chuckles. One of his hands glides over my shirt to rest at the base of my neck as he nips at my earlobe. "Are you feeling better?" I don't say anything, but he feels me nod my head. "What time is it?" His voice is rough from sleep and it sends a wave of desire down my spine.

Sliding a hand under my pillow, I grab my phone, the light of the screen making me wince. My eyes squint, trying to see past the blaring light, "It's almost five."

He hums in approval, his other hand toying with the hem of my shirt. "Good. That means I still have time." Anticipation leaves me breathing hard, my heart steadily picking up speed.

"Time for what?" I whisper between breaths. The hand toying with my shirt slides up my stomach making goosebumps pop up on my skin.

"Oh," he breathes, his mouth trailing down my neck, a hand slipping beneath the band of my panties. "I think you know."

I could easily get addicted to this man. Hell, I might already be.

"I thought you said not tonight." My back arches, my butt grinding against his hardening cock as his fingers slick between my folds. "Anson," I gasp as he sinks one finger deep into my pussy before withdrawing and lightly circling my clit.

"That was then, this is now," he whispers as he continues to tease me, "You're ready for me, aren't you?" I can feel him shifting behind me, but my only focus is on his fingers. My hips move in time with his fingers, the pleasure ramping up with every sweep across the sensitive bundle of nerves. "Get naked. Now."

Yes. Sir.

Without hesitation, my arms peel my too-large shirt over my head as Anson rids me of my underwear. In no time at all, I'm laying beside him once more.

"Have you ever been taken like this, baby?" His hard cock presses against my backside, his large hand sliding under my thigh, lifting it so he can gain access to my wet pussy. From behind, his cock glides through my wetness, making me writhe against him.

"No." Our voices are barely whispers, completely aware that the walls are extremely thin and the crew is within earshot—hopefully, sound asleep.

Anson slides his arm under my torso, his large hand settling against my pounding heart. "Good," he growls before slowly, so slowly, his cock pushes into me, filling me up. I'm utterly surrounded by him. And I love it.

My hips push back against his, wanting to take him deeper, willing him to move. But he doesn't. My free arm reaches around him, resting on his hip, urging him on.

"You want more, don't you baby? My greedy girl." His teeth bite down on my earlobe, but he doesn't move.

The hand pressing against my chest moves to my nipple, his skilled fingers pulling and teasing them into hardened points. The sensation of being filled by him while he toys with my nipples has my muscles clenching around him, needing more of him. He groans when my pussy squeezes him once more and he finally gives in.

"Fuck, Hannah. You're so goddamn perfect for me. You and your perfect pussy are everything I need."

Anson finally moves, giving me everything I've wanted. His hand never strays from my nipple as he pushes in and out of me. He maneuvers my leg, holding it up to rest on his hip before his hand slips between my folds, gently circling my clit.

My whole body is turning into an overdrive of sensations. His deep moans of pleasure reverberate through my ears, sending me over the edge.

My climax rolls through me and I cry out in pleasure, forgetting everything but the ecstasy coursing through my body. Anson's hand clamps over my mouth trying to dampen the sounds I'm making, his thrusts picking up speed as he chases his release.

Anson buries his head in my neck, all the sexy sounds he makes as he comes going right into my ear, making my muscles pulse around him even more.

It's so fucking hot to hear how I'm affecting him.

We're both sweaty and panting as we come down from our orgasms. "Well, that was one hell of a way to start the day." I'll be feeling the effects of him pounding into me from behind all day as I work on the boat running errands for Keith.

I don't regret a damn thing.

He chuckles before kissing my neck. "I'll keep that in mind." He pulls himself out of me, making me wince, but not in a bad way. I feel empty without him.

Anson sees it, tuning my face towards him. "You alright, baby? Was I too tough on this pussy?" His large hand moves to cup my mound, drawing a whimper from me.

I roll over, tucking myself against his chest. "Don't act like you're concerned. You love it." His chest rumbles against my cheek as he laughs, his light dusting of chest hair rubbing against me. "Besides," I add, "I like it when you get all rough."

"Is that right?" His hand fists in my hair, pulling my face up to his. "God, I'm glad I couldn't stay away." With that, he captures my mouth in a searing kiss. He completely owns me and fuck do I want him to. With a deep moan, he breaks the kiss, sighing in frustration. "I've got to go. Keeran will be off anchor watch soon, and I have to be gone when she gets here."

As much as I want him to stay with me, I understand that we can't have anyone find out. Keeran wouldn't tell anyone, but we can't risk it. Anson can't risk it and I don't want to be the person that ruins his reputation.

He pulls me in for one more kiss before climbing over me, careful to not hit his head on the top bunk. I watch him in silence as he quickly dresses, smiling as he tosses my shirt back at me. He gives me one last kiss before checking the hall and quietly slipping out.

There are several hours before I have to get up for breakfast service, so I roll over and grab Henry, pulling him tightly to my chest. He's no replacement for the man that just left my bed, but he'll do for now.

When Keeran sneaks into our room thirty minutes later, I'm still awake. "Oh, shit, did I wake you up?"

"Nah," I say as I roll over to face her, "I woke up and couldn't fall back asleep." No need to tell her about the amazing sex I had that I can't stop thinking of, or the man who is quickly stealing my heart.

"In that case," she perches on the edge of my bed, "you'll never fucking guess what happened tonight." She's in full gossip mode and I love a bit of juicy gossip.

"Lay it on me." I sit up and adjust Henry in my lap, careful to keep my naked bottom half under the covers.

"Guess who hooked up?"

Oh. Shit.

There's no way she could know about Captain and me, right? I trust him to be discreet, but there's only so much you can do on a boat.

Schooling my features, hoping my face doesn't betray my emotions, I swallow hard. "Oh my god, who?"

Keeran sits up and points directly at herself. "This girl." She bites her lip, her whole face beaming.

"Shut up," I gasp. "With who?"

Keeran blushes, wiping her hair out of her face. "Robbie."

"Oh my god, you have to tell me everything." Call me a gossip, but shit, do I love hearing all the details.

"Okay, so," Keeran pulls her legs up onto my bed getting ready to spill all the juicy details. "I took over the anchor watch from him, and we flirted a bit, of course." I nod my head in agreement and gesture for her to continue. "I made my rounds around the boat like I'm supposed to do. Except Robbie didn't go to bed. He was getting into the hot tub and damn does he have a good body. Anyway, he calls me over to him, which, you know, I can't resist. And he kisses me. Just grabs me by the neck and kisses the shit out of me."

"Damn. So where did you guys hook up then?" I'm even more impressed with Anson sneaking down here without being seen.

"The laundry room." She lets out a giddy squeal. "Han, it was *so* good. Let me just say, he knows what he's doing."

We talk about her and Robbie until my alarm goes off. I don't even mind that I'll be exhausted today from lack of sleep. It's been one eventful night.

Chapter Ten

Anson

The smell of coffee wafts its way up the stairs and I know that Hannah's awake. She's the most dedicated stewardess I think I've ever worked with, and I'm not saying that because I'm obsessed with her— she's truly amazing.

Soft footsteps bring a smile to my face because I know it's Hannah. Hannah, my personal siren who takes up my every waking thought.

"Good morning." Her voice is soft and gravelly, still a bit scratchy from sleep. Her long hair is down, cascading down her back like a waterfall as she brings me coffee.

Keith finally left the boat yesterday and I felt Hannah's tension float away the farther he got from the *Siren*. As busy as he kept her, we haven't been able to sneak away as often as I'd like.

By the time she was able to go down for the night, she'd pass out.

Several nights I found myself wandering down to the crew quarters whenever Keeran was on anchor watch just so I could be with her. She'd roll over and snuggle into my chest, kissing it lightly before drifting off back to sleep.

I take the mug from her, our fingers lingering as I do. "Good morning, baby." With a crook of my finger, I motion for her to come closer, wanting to greet her with a kiss. Her blue eyes dart around the bridge, but we're completely alone. Tentatively she places her knee between my thighs on the captain's chair and leans over giving me her lips.

The moment our lips touch, I sigh in contentment. God, I've missed the taste of her on my lips.

My tongue brushes against her lips and she opens for me, her tongue teasing mine. She tastes sweet, most likely from all the creamer she puts into her coffee each morning. She hums softly in her throat and my body immediately responds to that sound sending shivers down my spine.

Hannah leans further into me, her arms wrapping around my shoulders as she deepens our kiss.

"Captain Pike?" Grace Olivier's gentle voice floats up the stairs and into the bridge as the sun begins to rise over the horizon.

In an instant, the bubble created by Hannah is destroyed.

How could we be so careless?

Hannah immediately leaps away from me, her face white as a sheet. To distract myself, I lift the coffee Hannah brought to my lips, praying like hell Grace didn't see anything.

Grace rounds the corner at the top of the steps looking poised and unconcerned.

"Good morning, Dr. Olivier. Is everything okay?" My voice is calm while my nerves are on edge.

"I had a quick question if you have the time. Oh, good morning, Hannah." A smile I've only seen her give Hannah crosses her face. It's sweet and reminds me of a grandmother looking at her granddaughter.

Hannah has already started walking towards the steps and away from me wringing her hands. "Good morning, Grace. I didn't know you were up. Is there anything I can get for you?"

Grace waves her off. "Heavens no. I'll be fine for a bit longer."

Hannah nods her head, lightly touching the older lady's shoulder. "I'll be around when you need me." With one last worried glance back at me, Hannah jogs down the steps.

"What can I help you with?" She's been nothing but pleasant this whole time, and the crew has been keeping up to my standards, so I'm curious if there's an issue I need to address.

Grace slides onto the bench behind me as I turn my chair to face her. "My husband and I have noticed all of the hard work the crew, and you, have been putting in." She pauses, giving me a polite smile. "Well," she starts, "we wanted to give them a day off."

During a typical charter season, it's normal for owners to give the crew a day off every once in a while. There could be a day or two between charters that the owners use to show their appreciation to their employees. But this isn't a normal charter season, and we aren't running multiple charters, so I'm surprised.

"I'm sure they would enjoy that."

She nods as she links her hands on the table between us. "I agree. Mark and I know that it takes a lot of work to keep things running smoothly and everyone has been so wonderful." She pauses before continuing, "As you know, we are planning to see some friends in New Providence. We are planning on staying overnight with them and won't be returning to the boat until the next day." I nod, aware of their plans. "So, we want the crew to go out and have fun. We booked day passes for all the crew at the Bahama's Resort. We got one for you as well if you would like."

As generous, and tempting as that is, I have to stay with the boat. The thought of Hannah being able to lounge by the pool and relax is enough. She deserves every good thing that comes her way.

"Thank you, Dr. Olivier. I'll tell the crew. I know they've enjoyed working for you and your husband."

She stands and offers her hand, and I grasp it gently. "You really are doing a wonderful job," she praises. "We were saddened by Captain Lewis' retirement, but I don't think we could have found a better captain." With a quick thanks, she walks out of the bridge.

After the last couple of days, I know the crew needs some kind of pick-me-up after the havoc Keith caused.

The man wouldn't do anything for himself. He constantly sent food back for the chef to remake to his liking, had Hannah running back and forth with every small request, and even had Garrett's hackles rising with how he treated the deck crew. It's a wonder no one went off on him.

It's a few hours before I fill the crew in on their surprise for tomorrow. Most of the crew are up and working on the boat and Hannah is finishing up with breakfast service.

"All crew, all crew," I call into the radio, "meet me in the crew mess in ten minutes."

Hannah's the last one to enter the crew mess, no doubt having just come from our guests. Garrett stands and offers his seat to her, and I think again at how good of a first mate he's been.

"I've just spoken with Grace, and she and Mark are giving you guys a day off tomorrow."

Everyone's faces are a mixture of shock and pure relief. Hannah and Keeran high-five and the guys pat each other on the back. The small movement of Robbie's hand to the small of Keeran's back doesn't escape my notice.

"They paid for day passes for all of you to spend the day at the Bahama's Resort. You'll spend your day however you would like, but you will be back on the boat after dinner. The Oliviers are planning to stay with friends but will be back in the morning, so I expect you to be on deck at your normal hours."

A chorus of 'Yes, Captain' rings out as they all cheer and plan for a day of relaxation. Feeling eyes on me, I turn and look at Hannah who has a longing look in her eye. I have a feeling she's going to ask me if I'm going and I can't stand the thought of telling her no.

So badly I want to spend the day basking in the sun with her, splashing and playing in the cool water, to have an adventure together. But it can't happen. It *won't* happen, especially not with the rest of the crew around.

Ever so slightly I shake my head, answering her silent question. Disappointment flickers across her face, her forehead crinkling in the way I love before Keeran steals her attention.

Garrett's hand slaps my shoulder, his usually stoic expression is now one of happiness. "You're coming too, right Captain?"

My gaze lingers on Hannah for a moment longer. She's laughing with Keeran, the two of them no doubt making plans for tomorrow.

"I'm afraid not," I sigh as I drag my eyes away from her. "Someone has to stay on the boat." As if tethered to her, my eyes again find Hannah, her long hair pulled back into a ponytail hanging over her shoulder. "I might be able to stop by for a while. I'll see what I can work out."

"Good," he says, patting me on the shoulder while he takes a sip of coffee. "It'll be nice to see everyone off the boat, help the morale."

With a huff, I push myself up from my seat and head back to the bridge, the sounds of Hannah's laughter following me as I go.

• • • •

I'M IN A SHIT MOOD. The crew is bustling around as happy as can be, and here I am pissed off that I can't be with Hannah.

Time with her is quickly dwindling and now I'll have to spend a whole day away from her. While she's in a bikini.

Fuck.

My fists clench in frustration at the image of her sunbathing, her ass oiled up and glistening in the sun. But it was a close call this morning and we can't take any more risks than we are.

"Hey there, Captain." Joe, this ship's engineer, takes a seat in the bridge, letting out a huff. "Not as young as I used to be," he manages between heaving breaths.

"Oh, I don't know, Joe. You look like you've got a couple of years left in you." Joe's an old-school hard worker. He's either sleeping or in the engine room, almost like he's part of the ship.

His weathered face breaks out into a toothy grin. "Might have some juice left in these old bones still."

Every afternoon, Joe makes his way up from the bowels of the ship to have our afternoon chats. The man has some amazing stories and I enjoy listening to his knowledge.

He drags a hand down his bald head and leans back comfortably in his seat.

YES, CAPTAIN

"What adventures will you share today?" I ask. Our daily talks sometimes involve work, but mostly it's two men exchanging stories.

He thinks for a moment, rubbing his chin as he does. "How about my greatest achievement?" His face is solemn, no longer smiling or cheerful. Our talks are never serious, but I get the feeling today will be different. His weathered gaze meets mine and I nod for him to continue.

"Did I ever tell you I was married?" The gold ring on his finger catches my eye.

"No, I don't believe you have."

"Her name was Vera." His voice cracks at her name, the look in his eyes going distant as if he's picturing her in his mind. "We were married for thirty years. Today is our anniversary." His chin wobbles slightly and he clears his throat. "She was my greatest adventure."

The energy in the room shifts as the tough man in front of me fights back tears and breathes deeply. Part of me wants to ask what happened to her but out of respect, I won't push him.

After a few moments, he sniffles and clears his throat. "I'll tell you something, Anson. As a man who has spent most of his life at sea and squandered what he had when he had it, when you find that woman who settles your soul, you hold on tight and never let go. All the boats, all the seas... nothing will compare to the adventures you share with her. You hear me?"

His impassioned plea has me fighting to keep my composure. "Loud and clear."

Chapter Eleven

Hannah

S crew cleaning toilets, this is the life.

Ask anyone what got them into yachting and the majority of the time their answer will be wanting to see the world and make a lot of money. Which, yes, is true, but the other big reason for me is the perks. And shit, this is a pretty fucking good one if I say so myself.

It feels like it's been forever since I've seen the sun with so much time spent below deck, away from the sun's warmth. My skin is slathered with tanning lotion as I'm hoping to regain the tan that I've seemed to have lost in the time I've been on board.

The resort is *amazing* and after the shit Keith put me through, this is exactly what I need. Well, not exactly. The only thing that could make this day better is Anson and his big—

"Hannah! C'mon." Keeran yells at me from the middle of the pool with Robbie grabbing her waist from behind.

"Get your ass in the pool." Robbie playfully splashes the crystal-clear water in my direction. Little do they know that nothing could pry me out of this lounge chair.

Well, maybe one thing...

"Nah, I'm good here. I've got to get rid of my pasty ass." Keeran throws her head back in laughter, her blond hair dipping into the water.

"We'll be at the bar when you're ready." She pulls Robbie by the arm as he sticks his tongue out at me, which I return.

With no more distractions, I pull out my phone and dial Tiffany's number. Of course, we've been in constant contact since I snuck out the morning I came to the *Siren* without waking her up. A hung-over Tiff is not someone I want to deal with. Ever.

"For fuck's sake I thought you had forgotten all about me."

"What a lovely way to greet your best friend," I laugh. "You act like we haven't spoken in years."

"You've gotta admit you've been like the walking dead. You're there in body, but the mind is all blank."

"If you must know, I'm lounging in one of the top-rated resorts in the Bahamas right now. Zombie no more." I lean my head back against the headrest of the lounger and sigh. "It's paradise."

"Ugh, lucky bitch."

"How's the new boat? Getting along any better with the chief stew?" Last week was her first week on a new yacht for the summer and from what she's told me, her chief stew has it out for her.

Sheets rustle on the other end of the line. "She's an ice queen, but she has to put up with me. You caught me on my first break all day and I need some gossip that doesn't include me." Tiffany loves a good gossip session and I have this need to talk to someone about Anson.

My head turns on a swivel, my eyes searching out for any crew members close enough to overhear.

Damon and Garrett went down to the private beach and I'm pretty sure Damon's goal is to be Garrett's wingman. He's been joking that Garrett is too stiff and has been wanting to hook him up. Keeran and Robbie are making out in the pool under a palm tree, and Aidan is nowhere to be found. I even go so far as to sit up and look behind me, because this shit *cannot* get out.

"Okay," I whisper into the phone, "I've got something to tell you, but you can't tell anyone under any circumstances."

Tiff chuckles. "Damn, what's going on on that boat?" She's whispering back to me, making me smile.

"So... um..." The words aren't coming and I'm not sure where to start. "Let me just say that this boat has probably the best-looking crew I've ever seen in my life."

"Jealous." I ignore her comment and keep talking.

"Well, I told you that Captain Lewis retired, and his replacement is the sexiest man. Like ever. Anyway, so on day—"

"Oh my god," she gasps. "You're sleeping with the captain? Please, Han, say you're sleeping with him." She's downright giddy and I can picture her sitting up and bouncing in her bed.

I glance around once more checking for any crew members and cup my mouth over the speaker with my hand. "Yes, I'm sleeping with him." Her screams are so loud that I have to pull the phone away from my ear until she gets herself under control.

"Tell me *everything*," she begs. Some details I keep to myself, but I fill her in on some key details about how we got together, careful to not overshare.

"I'm confused though," I admit to her once I've dodged her questions. "We have only a few days left on the boat, but we haven't talked about anything that comes after."

"Maybe you need to." Her excitement has died down and she's not as hysterical. "Sneak into his room or something and ask him outright. He's a grown-ass man, he can tell you what he wants."

"Yeah," I sigh. "You're right." My fingers toy with the string of my bikini, noticing a tan line starting to form.

"Of course, I am," she quips. "But Hans, I've got to go. Ice bitch will ream my ass if I don't show up on time. Bye, babes."

Placing my phone on the table next to me, I lower the lounge chair and lay down on my front, reaching awkwardly behind me to untie my top.

The warmth of the sun's rays has my eyes sliding closed, my mind whirring.

Maybe Tiffany is right. Maybe I should sneak into his room and talk with him about it. It's not like we've had a ton of time to meet one on one with everything that's gone on this past week. Although the favorite part of my day was going to bed alone and waking up with him beside me. Now it's like I've programmed myself to search out for him in the middle of the night, even when I know Keeran is asleep above me.

In several weeks, I've come to need him in a way that I haven't needed anyone else. Yes, he fulfills me sexually that even the thought of him has my nipples pebbling, but it's a need that's deeper than anything. A soul-deep longing for him that's unlike anything I've ever experienced.

There's been a void in my life since Dad's death and I always thought it would be there. That I would be walking through life with this hole in my heart where only he could fit.

Until Anson.

How the hell has he wiggled his way in there? How has he gotten so far under my skin that even now, I feel his presence with me?

"Captain!" Robbie's shouting has me sitting up, stunned.

"Didn't think I'd ever see those, love." Leaning over on my elbow, I look over to see Damon and the guys grinning like fools.

Somewhere between the time I got off the phone to now, everyone has returned from wherever they were and has now all seen my breast.

At least Joe isn't here.

Garrett, like the gentleman he is, immediately turns his back to me. Aidan chuckles beside him looking anywhere but at me. And Anson? Anson stands behind my lounge chair and has a prime view of my exposed tits. Not that I mind him seeing them, it's felt like an eternity since he's touched them, but in front of the crew? Very bad idea.

As quickly as I can, I slam my body back down on the lounger, managing to bite my tongue when my chin bounces against the padding. I let out a pained groan as I fumble for the string of my bikini top.

"Are you alright, Hannah?" Anson walks over to Damon, Garrett, and Aidan, his voice full of concern.

I'm not sure what I'm expecting him to do in this situation. *I'm* not sure what to do when almost all the men I work with on a daily basis just got a free titty show at my expense. Crawl into a hole somewhere?

"Um, yeah, I'm fine," I stammer. "Just forgot my top wasn't on." Trying to not look embarrassed by my blunder, I turn and look at the group of men shrugging my shoulders. "It's just my tits, no big deal."

Once I have my top *securely* in place, I sit up, immediately reaching for my coverup from my bag. Anson's right hand is locked in a fist, his knuckles turning white with the force of it, but he otherwise looks unshaken.

"I'm glad you could get away from the boat for a bit to join us," Garrett says with a nod, blessedly changing the subject.

Anson clears his throat, his free hand adjusting his sunglasses. "Yeah, Joe almost shoved me off the boat himself, stubborn old man that he is."

"Well, Captain, we're glad you're here." Damon reaches over, patting him on the shoulder. "Let's have a drink."

• • • •

I'M DRUNK. A TERRIBLE decision, really. The pool bar and I are well acquainted now based on the number of fruity drinks I've shoved down my throat.

And it was all for nothing.

Anson had gone off with the guys to do who knows what, but the electric current zipping through my system at seeing him off the boat and in a delicious tank top showing off his sculpted chest and bulging biceps had me looking for any sense of relief, and I thought alcohol would do the trick.

It didn't. It makes everything a thousand times worse.

Especially when he took off the top and got into the water to toss a football with the guys. Keeran was looking longingly at Robbie, and it took everything in me to not drool at Anson.

Which led to more alcohol.

The sun is finally setting on our day at the resort, its orange glow signaling our dinner reservation is closing near.

"Alright guy," Anson says with a sigh as he glances at all of us. "I'm afraid it's time for me to leave." A chorus of complaints rings out from the guys, who have apparently had a man-bonding session today. They all look like kicked puppy dogs, which in my drunk state, I find hilarious.

"Look at their faces! Oh my god, this is so funny," I gasp between heaving bouts of laughter. My head falls to Keeran's shoulder causing my ass to slip off the seat altogether.

"Oh my god," Keeran breathes as she grabs me, hauling me back onto my seat before I sink completely into the water. "Damn girl, how much did you drink?"

Giggles still wrack my body, making it hard to breathe. "The whole bar's worth," I manage to slur, only slightly.

A man's deep voice calls over to us and it sends shivers down my spine. "Is everything okay over there?"

Drink in hand, I turn and face Anson, waving my drink at him. "Yes, Captain," I say extra cheery knowing full well just how much he loves to hear me say that. I admit, I want some sort of reaction from him that shows me that he's not unaffected by my presence, but the man is the picture of control.

His mouth lifts into an easy grin. "You ladies have fun." Keeran gives him a thumbs up as Anson turns to the guys. "Be back on the boat after dinner." With a wave, he turns and leaves without a glance back at me, and I'm hurt.

Part of me knows that we can't let others know what we are to each other—whatever it is *we* are. There's too much at stake for us to act on our feelings in public, but it doesn't dull the pain it brings me. Maybe I'm too invested in this.

Or he's not invested enough.

That sobering thought follows me to dinner. Everyone's laughing and having a good time, but I'm stewing in my feelings.

Aidan pays for a round of tequila shots and I all too willingly throw it back. It doesn't matter that I've had enough alcohol, I'll do anything to dull the ache in my chest. I'm so desensitized to the alcohol at this point that I don't even feel the burn of it as it slides down my throat.

When dinner is over, we load into the vans and head back to the boat. Keeran and Robbie walk arm-in-arm and I'm full of jealousy at how easy it is for them. There's no rule saying they can't be a couple or sleep together. They don't have to sneak around or hide from everyone. They know exactly where they stand with one another while Anson and I are in limbo.

Keeran turns and holds her hand out to me. "C'mon, Hannah. Walk with us."

Garrett, who has been walking beside me, grabs my arm to steady me as I lose my balance in my heels. I changed into a slinky dress and heels for dinner and now I'm regretting it, just like I always do on nights when I go out and drink too much.

Carefully, I quicken my steps to catch up with them, reaching for her outstretched hand. She pulls me close, resting her head on my shoulder as we walk.

"Robbie and I are going into a guest cabin tonight," she whispers into my ear, her voice full of anticipation.

"I am *not* cleaning up after you two," I snort. I'm all for her getting some dick tonight, but there's no way in hell that I want to be the one to strip the sheets.

She playfully nudges my shoulder as she barks out a laugh. "You don't have to worry. I'll clean the entire room and throw everything in the wash before you have to even ask."

When we reach the gangway, I remove my shoes and clutch Aidan and Damon's shoulders for dear life. It'd be just my luck to drunkenly fall into the water and that's something I wish to avoid.

Keeran and I hold each other's hands as we carefully take the steep steps down to the crew quarters, scared that we'll slip and fall making Aidan roll his eyes as he follows after us. She stops in our room briefly before joining Robbie with an excited hop to her step leaving me all alone.

For someone who has had a lot of alcohol—and I mean a lot—I'm surprised that I'm able to get into my oversized sleep shirt without falling over. With one last stop in the bathroom to wash my face and brush my teeth, I fall into my bed, which suddenly feels too big without Anson beside me.

I miss him.

All I wanted to do today was spend all day with him but couldn't. To lay in the sun together, flirt under the shade of the palm trees, and share drinks and laughter at the bar. But we couldn't.

Instead, he spent time bonding with the guys while I spent it trying to forget his touch.

Henry does little to comfort me as I hug him close to my chest and pray my eyes slide shut. But they don't. All I can think about is Robbie and Keeran and how they have each other, while I'm left with my Squishmallow pinning for my captain.

I've had enough of stewing in my head for one day.

With a flourish, I rip the sheets from my body and stealthily ease my way into the hallway. Part of me feels like one of those old cartoons with the bad guys tip-toeing through corridors dramatically, but that's what I'm doing. The thought has me stifling a giggle.

The crew mess is all clear and a little pang of excitement zings through my body.

Holy shit this is going to work.

As gracefully as possible in my drunken state, I gently ease my way up the steps to the main salon. My fists are white as I hold on to the railing for dear life because it would be just my luck to slip and tumble down the steep steps.

All hope is dashed the second I turn the corner at the top of the steps. Voices. Lots of male voices are coming from the bar.

Of course, the guys would still be drinking. It's our only day off, so everyone's taking complete advantage while we can. We've got to let off steam in one way or another and I know for a fact they aren't getting laid.

Well, except for Robbie.

As I see it, I have two options. I can try to run for the galley and up the steps to Anson's room, or I could call the whole thing off. I've already made it this far, might as well make a run for it.

Doing my best Captain Jack Sparrow impersonation, I dodge through the hallway and across to the galley, feet slapping lightly on the tile floor.

Oh my god, I've made it. I can't believe I'm just as sneaky as that sexy bastard.

Out of pure thrill, excited tingles travel up my spine and I can't contain my joy any longer. Letting out a small squeal, I throw my hands in the air in triumph, my feet stomping back and forth as I do my little jig. Hair from my messy ponytail slides in front of my face with my movement but I don't care. I'm too damn happy about my ninja skills.

"Love? What are you doing?" Damon's teasing laughter halts my movements.

I can honestly hear the record scratch in my head. If ever there was a time for one, it's now.

Confusion muddles its way through me as my brain catches up. I admit it takes longer than I would like, but I blame the alcohol for that.

I'm winded from my impromptu dance, my breath coming out in puffing pants making my curtain of hair part with every exhale. Pulling my hair away from my face, I see Damon leaning against the refrigerator, a charming grin on his face. He's holding a container of ice cream and playfully licks the spoon as he watches me.

"Oh," I pant, looking around for any excuse for my actions, "I was excited about ice cream," I lie.

Damon eyes me suspiciously, clearly not believing my lie, but he doesn't call me out on it. "Okay," he says, "Which flavor?" He steps back and opens the door. "We've got chocolate, vanilla, cookies n' cream..."

"That one," I spout as quickly as possible.

"You're going to have to be more specific, love." He leans back and gives me a crooked smile.

My hands fidget with the hem of my shirt, shuffling nervously on my feet. "Cookie n' cream," I answer as footsteps come up from behind me, making me turn.

"Oh, hey. We're getting ice cream?" A hand slides across my upper back as Aidan squeezes behind me and into the galley. He's damp and wearing swim trunks; no doubt having come from the hot tub. "Toss me a vanilla, would ya?" He holds up his hand and Damon tosses it right to his waiting palm. "Sweet, thanks."

Damon hands me the small container and I quickly search for a spoon. This might not be what I had planned but damn does ice cream sound good.

"You coming to join us, Hannah?" Aidan reaches around me for a spoon quickly popping a dollop of sugary goodness into his mouth.

"You know, I think I might," I manage to say around my own spoonful. I'm already up, so I might as well have some fun.

Chapter Twelve

Anson

A high-pitched feminine screech has my eyes opening. The clock on the built-in nightstand says it's well after midnight, meaning the crew is on board, and from the sound of it, they're still enjoying their day off.

With a heavy groan, I drag myself upright, my feet hitting the cold floor of the cabin. Again, a sharp squeal and men's laughter reach my ears. It's too late for them to be messing around, especially when they are expected to maintain their normal work hours.

I don't bother tossing on a shirt and make my way through the side door of the bridge and out onto the teak of the gangway. There's another scream accompanied by the sound of splashing water that has me quickening my steps until the hot tub comes into view.

What the hell are they doing?

Hannah spurts up from the bottom of the hot tub, a large smile caressing her cheeks as she laughs. Her long hair is slicked back from the water, and she looks as breathtaking as ever. Sitting on the edge of the hot tub are Damon and Aidan, both laughing. Aidan clutches his stomach as Damon holds onto his shoulder like he'll fall over in a fit of laughter if he didn't.

"I think that was the best one!" Hannah wipes the water from her eyes as she stands, climbing onto the seats of the hot tub and sitting beside Damon on the lip, their feet resting in the water below.

Hot flames of jealousy surge through my veins as I watch him reach across her back and rest his hand on her hip.

Hannah's not wearing a swimsuit. I easily recognize the oversized gray t-shirt she likes to sleep in and she's wearing nothing but bright pink underwear that peeks out from under the hem. The drenched shirt sticks to her skin leaving little to the imagination.

"What the hell is going on?" My words come out harsh with anger, startling the happy trio.

Aidan stands and tries to turn quickly, his feet slipping in the water, and he stumbles forward catching himself on the lip of the hot tub with an outstretched arm.

"Shit," he curses as he rights himself. "We were just, uh..." His eyes glance over to Damon who appears to be the least intoxicated of the three. Hannah was almost drunk when I left them before dinner and there's an open beer sitting beside her on the ledge, telling me she's been drinking all this time.

What the hell is she thinking?

"Having a good time," Damon finishes for him. "But we're heading off now, right mate?" He slaps Aidan on the chest, and he nods in agreement. Damon offers his hand to Hannah, who looks over at me with wide eyes.

Before she can link her hand with his, I step forward. "I'll take care of Hannah. You two get to bed. I expect you to be on deck on time."

Hannah reaches for my hand and slides her legs over the edge of the hot tub, water splashing on the teak. Without thinking, my free arm reaches around her and lifts her off it, placing her on her feet in front of me. She wobbles unsteadily and clutches my side in an attempt to right herself.

Both men watch us with confused expressions. "Hannah, you good?" Aidan watches her face carefully and she smiles over at him.

"Perfect," she slurs as she gives the men a thumbs up. "Thanks for tonight. It was so much fun." She runs a hand down my naked chest, completely unconcerned by our audience.

"Right," Damon drawls, his eyes watching Hannah's hand as she runs it back and forth along my skin. "I'll check on you in the morning, love." He tilts his head in my direction, "Captain." Damon taps Aidan on the shoulder, nudging him along through the doors to the main salon.

"Bye, guys," Hannah calls after them as she wraps her arms around me and waves at the retreating men. Once they're gone, she looks up at me, her arms linked around my waist. "Hello, Captain." She smiles up at me, her blue eyes glinting in the light and I can't help but think how everything is about to be turned upside down.

Damon and Aidan now know our secret.

My smile is tight and forced, my stomach clenching in a knot. "Let's get you taken care of, baby. Can you walk?"

"Ha!" she cries, "Can I walk?" As if I issued her a challenge she won't back down from, she holds her arms wide taking quick steps back as if to say, '*Look at me.*' She manages two steps before she wobbles, and I reach out quickly to steady her.

Not wanting her to hurt herself, I hoist her easily into my arms. Hannah lets out a surprised yelp before wrapping her arms around my neck and nuzzling her face in the crook of my shoulder.

"I missed you today," she murmurs quietly as I carry her through the boat. Her soft lips gently kiss my skin and I hold her body closer to me. I don't care that she's drunk or that her shirt is soaking wet. What matters is that she's in my arms.

"I missed you too, baby," I admit, pressing a kiss to her forehead. "Did you have fun today?"

One small hand slides down from around my neck, her fingers running through my chest hair as she sighs. "I would've had more fun with you," she says regretfully. "I was trying to come and see you, you know."

"What do you mean?" I ask as we pass by the galley door and to the steep stairs leading to the crew area.

"I was trying to be a ninja and sneak up to your room. Wake you up," she pops the P and giggles to herself. "But," she sighs, "Damon caught me doing my happy dance, so I drank."

I'm not sure what a happy dance is, but I understand what she's saying. She was coming to see me and to avoid being found out, she stayed with Damon and Aidan. While I would have preferred her to go back to her bed, I don't voice it.

Maybe I should teach her a lesson later. I think we'd both like that.

Turning sideways down the small hallway to not hit her feet, I carefully open the door to her shared bedroom like I've done many times before. Keeran's top bunk is empty, and I thank God for tiny miracles.

At least that's one less person who will know about us.

"She's sleeping with Robbie," Hannah whispers in my ear as I set her on her bed. Her eyes are growing heavy, her arms limp at her sides. She wouldn't have lasted much longer in that hot tub.

"Do you have any water in here?" Her and Keeran's room is a cluttered mess with clothes littering every surface. She points to her nightstand, and sure enough, there's a full bottle. I open the top and hand it to her. "Drink it all."

She giggles, her eyes sliding shut. "Soo bossy," she complains, but she does as she's told, lifting it to her mouth and swallowing the contents. Once she reaches the bottom, she holds the empty container out to me. "Happy?"

Chuckling, I take it from her. "Thank you, baby. Now, arms up." Her eyes slowly open, looking at me in surprise. She looks around dramatically and motions me closer.

"Now? Anson, I think I'm too drunk for sex," she slurs, her hot breath tickling my ear.

"Hannah, your shirt is soaking wet. I'm not trying to have sex with you right now. Let's get you into some dry clothes and in bed so you can sleep."

I always want to have sex with Hannah, but not when she's drunk. I want her fully coherent when I sink my cock deep inside her.

"Ooh," she giggles before tossing both arms straight in the air. She forgets that she's on the bottom bunk and her arms thunk hard against the wood. "Oww," she whines while laughing through the pain.

Tenderly I check her injured hands kissing them softly before gripping the hem of her shirt and pulling it over her head, tossing it into the open bathroom door.

God, she's so fucking beautiful.

There's a shirt tossed at the end of her bed and I grab it, sliding it down over her head and shoulders.

"Stand up, baby." She holds her hands out to me, and I help her stand. "Gotta get these off too." She doesn't protest as my thumbs hook under the elastic and pull the water-logged panties down her legs hitting the floor with a wet slap. Slowly I lower her back down to the bed making sure she's stable before I hunt for some new underwear. I've been in this room enough times to know which closet is hers and easily find her stash of underwear and kneel before dragging them up her luscious legs.

Now that she's dressed in dry clothes, I cup her head as I lower her to the mattress, making sure she doesn't hit that precious head of hers. She moans softly when I press a kiss on her forehead.

"Stay with me." She grabs my arm, her eyes locking with mine. "Please?"

There was never any chance of me resisting her, I realize. Not now, not ever.

My fingers brush along her jaw, "Of course, baby." She puckers her lips and I honor her request, bending over and kissing her gently before crawling into bed behind her. "Now go to sleep." She sighs deeply, nestling against my chest.

While Hannah drifts off to sleep in my arms, I'm busy memorizing the feel of her next to me, breathing in the scent that lingers in her damp hair. The clock that's been ticking down since the moment she stepped onto this boat is quickly spiraling down, building momentum and plunging towards the end.

I can't control it. I can't control anything.

Damon and Aidan know about our relationship. They were both drunk, but not drunk enough to be blinded to how

Hannah responded to me. They might keep their mouths closed, but something in Damon's eyes hint otherwise, and I don't blame him. He and Hannah are close, I know that. If he thought anything untoward was going on, I have no doubt he'd report it. Hell, I would if I were in his position.

Hannah twitches next to me, moaning softly. "Henry," she whispers, "I need Henry."

My face scrunches in confusion. "Who is Henry, baby?" My hand runs up and down her side, offering comfort.

"My penguin," she mutters.

I've noticed the penguin stuffed animal many times and each time it's served as a stark reminder of our age difference.

Careful to not bang my head against the top bunk, I search her bed for the plush toy. Soft fabric brushes against my fingers and I pull Henry from behind my back and offer it to her.

Her sleepy hands pull it to her chest, and she sighs happily. "Hmm. I love you."

Heart hammering in my chest, it feels like all the air was sucked out of my lungs. Hannah's breathing quickly evens out, snoring softly with sleep. She very well could be talking about the stuffed animal she clings so tightly to her chest, but it doesn't make the feeling of those words any less potent.

My lips brush against her temple, my voice shaky and thick with emotion. "I love you too, baby." And I mean every word.

Chapter Thirteen

Hannah

Anson is distant.

He's not sitting in the captain's chair in the bridge when I bring him his morning coffee like he usually is. It's the only time of the day that we really have to ourselves and I know he looks forward to it every morning.

Not once has he asked me to bring him something to eat or drink, but this is something I want to do for him.

Instead, he's out on the bow of the boat, his strong back to me as he gazes out along the bay.

Last night was completely unplanned and when I awoke, pain pills and a bottle of water were waiting on the nightstand.

The whole night is a blur for the most part with only bits and pieces sticking in my memory. After Damon caught me in the act, the three of us drank in the hot tub which eventually led to some sort of falling competition. Of course, it's dumb as shit to do that in a hot tub but blame the fucking alcohol.

I'm not as hungover as I should be, and I know I have Anson to thank for that.

Vaguely I remember Anson carrying me to bed and holding me as I drifted off to sleep. I also remember saying those three little words.

Not one part of me wants to take them back.

Maybe that's what's made him so introspective.

Unsure of whether he wants to be disturbed, I place the steaming mug on the table and search for a pen and paper. I jot down a quick good morning note and leave it under his mug,

SIERRA SHIPLEY

the thought of him reading it as he picks up his coffee makes me happy.

He makes me happy.

He was so sweet and gentle last night as he took care of me. Tiff says that I'm terrible and needy when I drink too much, but Anson didn't act like I was. Maybe that's in the parts I don't remember and I hope it stays that way.

The Oliviers are returning from their overnight stay later this morning and then we depart for our return trip. We'll stop at some ports along the way, but our three weeks are coming to a close.

Since we were gone all day yesterday, there's a lot that needs to get done before Grace and Mark arrive. Stopping for a quick sip of my morning coffee, I take the stairs down to the guest cabins. I haven't seen Keeran this morning, so I'm assuming she and Robbie are still enjoying their time together.

Good for them.

I work quickly to strip the sheets in the master cabin and scrub the bathroom clean. They're probably going to want some relaxation time, so I add double towels and set out a face mask for Grace.

After working for some time, my stomach lets out a long, low growl. Damon should be awake by now and working on crew breakfast. My mouth waters at the thought of a warm muffin topped with melting butter.

"Morning, cheffy," I sing as I step into the galley. His back is to me, the sound of bacon sizzling and the smell of them cooking on the grill has me moaning. "Whatcha cookin' up for us today?" I ask as I plop myself onto the countertop and watch him work, sipping at my now cool coffee.

He doesn't turn around, but calls over his shoulder, "Hannah, love, can we have a little chat?"

"If you're wanting to talk about your major loss to me last night, then you'll be sorry. I won that round fair and square." Aidan had been the judge on our first round of hot tub sports, and he clearly stated that I was the winner. I *think*.

He chuckles and reaches for the nob of the stove, lowering the heat before turning to me. "Nah, it's non-contested." He placed both palms on the counter across from me, the only space between us being the small walkway. "I wanted to talk with you about last night." His voice is lower and has a more serious ring to it. We're normally fun, flirty banter, but this is different.

My hand grasps the handle of the mug beside me, bringing it to my mouth. "Okay?"

"What's going on between you and the captain, love?" His blue eyes skewer into me, full of concern. My sharp intake of air has the liquid going down the wrong pipe, and I cough uncontrollably while he stands there watching me.

How does he know?

My mind sifts through garbled memories of last night and nothing comes to mind. We were laughing and having fun, and then Anson showed up. He carried me to bed and stayed the night with me.

Wait... *he carried me to bed*. Were Damon and Aidan there when he picked me up? For the life of me, I can't remember.

Damon sighs and turns back to the stove, flipping over rows of bacon before turning back to me when my coughing subsides.

"What do you mean?" My first thought is to play dumb because I genuinely am at this moment. I'm not sure what he's alluding to, and I'm sure as hell not going to give myself away.

"I mean," he whispers, "the way you were rubbing all over him. It looked," he pauses, glancing around the small galley, "*familiar*. Like you've done it before."

"What?" I sputter, completely shocked. Did I lose my shit the moment Anson stepped on deck last night? It's one hundred percent possible. I'd been thinking of the man all day and I was drunk...

Fuck.

Damon holds his hands up apologetically. "It's not my business, love, but I wanted to check on you. Make sure you're alright."

I've ruined everything.

My hands begin to shake, terrible tremors that threaten to spill what little coffee is left in the mug. I'm panicking at the realization that something is going to happen, that I won't see Anson again, that one of us—or both—is going to get fired.

Shit, shit, *shit*.

"It's alright, love." Damon walks around the counter and gently takes the sloshing mug from my grasp, setting it next to me. His warm hands glide up and down my arms in comfort. "I'm not going to tell anyone."

He's not going to tell anyone. The thought repeats through my head, my heart rate slowing as I take deep, soothing breaths, letting them out slowly.

"T-thank you, Damon. I'm alright," I stammer, doing my best to sound convincing. "There's no need to worry about me. Or *that*," I add with a pointed look.

"Well, alright then." He pushes away from me and goes back to the stove, completely unfazed.

I've got to get out of here.

My body is on autopilot as I head down to my room. I need time to think.

Like a zombie, I sit on the edge of my bed and stare at the back of the door. We've tried so hard to keep everything a secret and in one tiny moment, I've ruined everything. My gaze goes unfocused, everything around me blurs and morphs as I dwell on the possibility of what happened last night.

Fuck alcohol—I don't think I can be trusted to drink again. Apparently, I ruin things when I do, like spilling secrets.

But Damon is my friend. He said he won't say anything to anyone, and I believe him. So why am I so worried?

It's all going to work out.

We're *fine*.

Mentally slapping myself out of my haze, I stand and get back to work. The phrase '*toughen up buttercup*' comes to mind. It was one of my dad's favorite lines whenever I complained about something, so it makes sense that it's what runs through my head now. He taught me to always look ahead and to push through the hard times, so that's what I'm going to do: push through.

Hunger completely replaced by unsettled nerves, I bypass the kitchen and the chef that occupies it and opt to get ready for Grace and Mark's arrival. Garrett comes on the radio announcing that he's meeting the Oliviers at the entrance of the harbor, which is odd, but not all that unusual. Garrett's one of those guys who seems to go above and beyond in everything he does.

It isn't long before familiar figures walk down the dock, Garrett behind them carrying their overnight luggage. I was expecting them to be all smiles after just seeing their friends, but their expressions are tight, forced. They both greet me with polite smiles, but there's something about their eyes that has me worried.

Neither one of their smiles reached their eyes.

"Hannah, dear, would you do me a favor and unpack my bag? I'd like to have the clothes washed as well." She takes the cool towel I offer, quickly wiping down the nape of her neck. The humidity has everyone looking like wet dogs and I'm tempted to grab one for myself.

"Absolutely," I smile kindly at the older woman as she walks past me and into the main salon. Mark follows closely after her, his hand on her lower back.

"I'll get these to their room for you, Hannah." Garrett sidesteps past me, luggage in both arms.

"Thanks," I say as I quietly check on Grace and Mark as we pass by them. Both of them have stopped at the water tray and arrangement of snack foods I placed at the bar, neither one looking like they need something.

Laundry it is.

By the time I emerge from my laundry cave, the energy on the boat is tense. Aidan sits in the crew mess, staring at his sandwich, his eyes distant and thoughtful, which is unlike him. We did drink a lot last night, so I'm guessing he's feeling his hangover pretty hard right now.

My arms are full of freshly pressed clothes that need to go straight to Grace's closet. The dresses she wears are beautiful and delicate and I don't want them to crease.

The door to their room is closed and I gently tap on it and wait for a response.

Mark opens the door, his smile tight. "Hey, kid. We've been waiting for you."

"Oh, really? Well, here I am," I force a smile and a laugh, trying to cut through whatever this odd tension is. The air just feels uncomfortable. It reminds me of when my parents were talking about me in front of me, but not *saying* they were talking about me. I hated it then and I hate the feeling I'm getting now.

"Have a seat, Hannah." Grace's voice is soft and cautious as she takes a seat in the small seating area and gestures to the open chair. Mark stands beside her, his hand resting on her shoulder.

This is fucking weird.

I carefully hang the garments in her closet before taking a seat. My hands start to feel clammy, and I squeeze my palms together. "Is everything okay?"

Grace sighs heavily. "We wanted to tell you that we had no idea that Captain Pike was like that. We are so sorry that we were blind to his advances. He's been removed from the boat and won't be returning."

My stomach drops. "What?" I stammer, breathless.

Mark gives Grace a reassuring squeeze, his gaze turning to mine. "We had no idea he would pursue a relationship with you. It's completely inappropriate. We're just sorry we didn't know sooner."

Grace leans forward, placing a cool hand on my knee. "Are you alright dear?"

No, I'm not fucking alright. Damon's a goddamn liar.

Anger boils through me, hot and devouring leaving nothing behind but sizzling rage. It takes every ounce of willpower to not lose my temper at the two people sitting across from me.

"No one took advantage of anyone," I say, as calmly and firmly as I can. "If you fired him, you might as well fire me too." My gaze locks with their faces, my chin set stubbornly.

Mark sighs, his head shaking. "He was your superior, Hannah. He took advantage. He knew better, yet still continued your relationship. He even admitted to it—took full responsibility."

That *asshole*.

"He can't take full responsibility when there are two people at fault," I argue. My anger and sense of professionalism are warring with each other, fully aware that I'm sounding like a petulant child.

"We'll give you some time to process this before the entire crew is informed." Grace completely ignores my argument, her eyes soft with concern.

With a huff, I leave their room and sprint to the bridge. If there's even a chance Ansons is still on board, then I'm going to take it. I don't know if I'll kiss him or punch him, or maybe both.

Both sounds good.

When I enter the bridge, the door to the captain's quarters is wide open. Every surface is wiped clean and polished, the bed has been stripped of its sheets all folded neatly on the end of the mattress.

Every trace of him is gone.

Chapter Fourteen

Anson

The phone rings again, with Hannah's name sprawled across the screen. I stare at it until it goes to voicemail, every muscle twitching with the need to answer.

I always let it go to voicemail.

It's better this way, I try to convince myself.

I never should have lost control with her. Should never have started this thing between us, and now it's time to make up for that mistake all those weeks ago.

I'm doing what I should have done in the first place.

Staying away.

But every fucking ring of the phone leaves me aching for her. The smell of coffee has me seeing her smiling face. The clear blue sky has me thinking about her eyes and how I miss staring into their beautiful depths.

She's better off without me, I remind myself. She needs to be young and free. She doesn't need me to hold her down.

But then the image of her arms bound as I look up the length of her glorious body before putting my mouth on her plays through my mind.

My siren likes to be bound. She likes to be controlled. Dominated.

But I lost control and now I pay the price.

Every day apart is torture. Torture I must endure.

Chapter Fifteen

Hannah

The *Siren* used to feel like home to me. Now it feels like a prison.

I can't wait to get off this mother freaking boat.

Anson and I never got the chance to talk about what happens after the boat and now he won't answer my calls. The moment I left his empty room, I called. Again, and again and again.

Nothing.

The crew doesn't help either. Everyone's walking on eggshells around me, acting like I'm a wounded little bird.

I'm not.

I'm pissed as hell.

Keeran's the only one who acts remotely normal around me. She understands what happened. That night she leaned over the edge of her bed, her hair dangling as she said, "I wish you would've told me. We had a deal!" before throwing her pillow down onto my face from her top bunk.

Damon, the traitor, I refuse to talk to which makes food service awkward. I jot down any requests in my notebook and slide it over to him. Yeah, it's childish as fuck, but I honestly don't care.

Aidan's been giving me puppy dog eyes the whole time but never says anything. Not that I want to talk to him right now. The only person I want to talk to won't answer the goddamn phone.

So, I'm brooding.

I've cocooned myself in a giant hoodie, tucked into the corner of the booth in the crew mess. It's not the best place to stew in my feelings, but my bed has become a harsh reminder of Anson and I can't deal with that right now.

I miss him. So much.

How is it that I miss someone I've known for just over two weeks?

Tiff tells me to move on, but she doesn't understand the raw connection we have. I don't think I could ever move on from him. He's buried himself in my goddamn heart.

Tears prick my eyes and I fight to keep myself under control.

"How you holdin' up, honey?" I wipe away the traitorous tears with the sleeve of my hoodie before glancing up. Joe fiddles around in a cabinet, no doubt searching for M&M's—the man's addicted.

I made the mistake of not ordering enough for him last year and he gave me dirty looks the whole time. He's a sweetheart though and was only giving me a hard time.

"I'm fine," I say, sniffling.

He glances over his shoulder, his bald head reflecting the overhead light with the movement. He doesn't look convinced in the slightest.

"I've seen that look many times. Felt it too." The cabinet door swings shut with a soft thud as Joe sits on the bench across from me tossing back his candy. "What's on your mind?"

Joe's a sweet old man and reminds me of my dad in a way. He's quiet and hardworking but is a big ole softy.

After Anson left, Garrett called all the crew for a meeting to explain the situation. He didn't go into great detail, but there aren't many other people Anson could've had an *inappropriate relationship* with, so it didn't take a genius to put the pieces together.

I felt everyone's eyes swivel to me, see them judging me, but not Joe. His eyes were soft and comforting. Understanding. He was there for me when my heart was hurting from losing my dad and today is no different. The heartache may not be the same, each with its own unique pain, but heartache is heartache.

"I guess the question should be what *isn't* on my mind," I whisper. My hands cover my face as I breathe deeply, pushing down any outward sign of emotion. When they slide away, Joe smiles at me.

"One of those, huh?" he asks, his voice gentle. "I know that all too well."

Emotion lays heavy in my throat making it impossible to respond. My throat works convulsively, attempting to rid myself of this feeling, but nothing helps.

Joe looks at me as if he wants to wrap his arms around me in a warm hug. The only person I want to hold me right now is Anson.

Hurt and longing flow through me in waves, the dam of tears in my eyes spilling over and gliding down my cheeks.

"You know," he starts, tossing back the last of his candies, "sometimes we push away the things that matter most to us. It's not right, or logical, but it's what we do when we think someone is better off without us." I sniffle and wipe tears away that just keep coming. Joe sighs, a soft smile tugging at the corners of his mouth. "Give him time. If he's anything like me, he'll come around."

He stands, reaching over and giving my shoulder a quick pat. "You're good for him, I can tell." He turns to leave but looks back at me with one foot on the stairs. "You remind me of my Vera," he says softly, before turning and walking back up the steps.

• • • •

IT'S FINALLY OVER.

These last few days of the charter have been non-stop. We stopped at various ports on the way back to Fort Lauderdale, but the worst was the impromptu beach picnic.

Mark spotted a beach that he just *had* to see. Which meant Damon raced to get food prepared and I about lost my mind trying to get all the materials for a picnic together. *By myself.* Keeran tried to help, but since she works on deck she didn't know her way around the interior.

The new captain doesn't help either.

Captain Rife is an older man who barely utters a word. He just looks at me with a disapproving look and never once bothered to help. He stood in the hallway outside the galley and watched me run around the main salon, a scowl on his face.

Prick.

Thank god I don't have to work for him anymore.

The Oliviers left the boat yesterday afternoon shortly after we docked. They were very generous and gave us all hefty tips that *almost* made up for all the shit I had to do for Keith.

Almost.

After that, it was the simple business of getting the boat cleaned so I could finally leave. Good riddance.

YES, CAPTAIN

Anson still hasn't returned any of what feels like hundreds of phone calls. Joe told me to give him time, that he'd come around, but he's nowhere in sight.

Keeran's already left, giving me a big hug and leaving with the promise to get together soon. I'm not sure where she and Robbie left things, but they left together. I just wonder how much longer it's going to last. Boat-mances rarely survive off charter.

Now all I have left is to shove my clothing that litters the floor into my bag and I'll be off this damned boat. I just want to get home and lay in my own bed, one that has no memory of Anson.

Just as I sit on top of my luggage in an attempt to get it closed, a sharp knock startles me. I'm winded from my wrestling match, my long hair sticking to my damp face.

Aidan nudges the door open farther, poking his head around. "Do you need help?" His eyebrows furrow at my predicament, a slight smile crossing his face.

"Um, yeah actually," I huff. "Be a doll and zip this for me?" I'm sure I look like a hot mess, but I give him my best smile hoping he'll take pity on me.

"Sure," he laughs, stepping completely into the tiny room and crouching in front of me. It's a bit awkward with him having to maneuver around my long legs, but the hissing sound as the zipper closes is music to my ears.

"Thanks," I say, trying gracefully to slide off the luggage without damaging it. "You leaving?"

He shrugs his shoulders, "Yeah. It's time to head home." I hop up and wrap my arms around his shoulders. I'm going to miss my friend. When I pull back, he glances around nervously, not meeting my gaze. "Hannah, I wanted to apologize."

My eyebrows knit together in confusion. Why does Aidan have to apologize?

"Okay..." I draw out the word until it sounds more like a question than a statement.

Aidan's large hand slides through his hair as he lets out a ragged breath. "It's my fault, not Damon's," he admits.

My stomach drops. I'm pretty sure my jaw drops too from shock. When I'm able to regain some of the breath I lost, I manage to stammer, "What?"

"I was still pretty hungover from that night," he rushes, "and when Garrett asked what we got up to, I let it slip that it looked like you and Captain had something going on. I should've known he'd do something about it. You know how he is," he pauses, his look pleading. "I'm so sorry, Hannah."

My head nods on autopilot as I try to sort through this new information. There's so much I'm trying to take in that I can't form a coherent thought. It was Aidan, not Damon that ratted us out. Now everything makes sense.

That morning Garrett escorted the Oliviers from the dock and when they stepped on the boat, I remember how they all looked tense, not like they had just had a good time with their friends.

Holy shit.

I back up until the back of my knees meets the mattress and I plop down. "I'm such an asshole," I mutter to myself. I've blamed Damon this whole time, been cold and terrible to him. "Why didn't you tell me before?" I ask, my eyes wide.

Aidan sits beside me. "I don't know," he sighs. "I felt terrible. Feel terrible, like a shit friend. I guess," he pauses, his large hands sliding through his hair once more, "I don't know, Hannah. I'm an idiot. But I wanted you to know it was my fault. I wanted to tell you before you left."

As much as I want to hit him, scream at him, *something*, I can't bring myself to do it. Nothing will change the past. Nothing will bring Anson back or undo the damage my anger toward Damon has caused.

"I wish you would have told me sooner."

"I know."

With a huff, I stand up and head for the door. "It looks like you're not the only one that has some apologizing to do today."

I find Damon in his shared room with Garrett rolling up his knives. I don't say a word, I just walk in and wrap my arms around his back.

"I'm so sorry," I mumble between his shoulder blades. "I know you didn't tell anyone about Anson and me. I should've believed you, and I'm sorry for that."

Damon chuckles, his laughter humming against my ear. "I know, love." His hand wraps around mine, gently pulling them apart so he can turn to face me. "You needed someone to be mad at. Still, you didn't have to be such a bitch about it," he teases playfully.

I sit on his bed as he meticulously packs his bags. Of course, he asks questions about Anson, which I do my best to evade, unable to think about him right now without crying.

Once he's all packed, we make our goodbyes with the remaining crew and exit, leaving the boat together.

My sandals clack against the concrete as I step off the boat with the help of Damon's steadying hand. He pulls me in for one last hug. "I'll miss you, love."

"Oh come on," I slap his chest playfully as I pull back, "You'll be calling the next girl my nickname in no time. Probably as soon as she steps into your galley."

Damon grins at me while sliding on his sunglasses and reaching for his bag. "I'll see you around, Hannah."

"Bye, cheffy," I murmur as I watch him walk away from me.

Chapter Sixteen

Anson

Everything is pointless when it comes to Hannah.

I have no sense of control or restraint when it comes to that beautiful girl that has captured my heart.

It's been hell ignoring every one of her goddamn phone calls, to the point that I had to put my phone on silent to keep from being tempted to answer. When those phone calls started to become less frequent, I thought my heart would rip from my chest.

So yeah, it was all pointless because now I'm standing on the dock holding a fucking stuffed animal. What is it called? Oh, yeah, Squishmallow.

I felt like a creep when I walked into the toy aisle and picked out one that I thought she would like. The squid-octopus-looking thing hangs in my hand as I watch her make her goodbyes with Damon.

She looks just as stunning as the day I first saw her walking on this dock. She's wearing shorts and a tank top, her long hair braided to the side. All I can see is her back as she watches Damon walk away and for a second, I think she's going to call after him.

After a moment, she grabs the handle of her bag and turns toward me. I expect her to see me, but her eyes never stray from her feet. I can tell the moment she spots me when her head lifts to take in her surroundings. Her sandal catches on the concrete, her arms flailing at her sides, saving her balance.

She's twenty feet away and my hand twitches with the need to touch her. To have her in my arms again.

She rights herself before locking eyes with me.

God, I've missed those eyes.

Hannah doesn't smile or run to me. She doesn't look happy to see me at all. She squares her shoulders and lifts her chin and walks toward me.

"Hannah." My voice is rough, my heart pounding nervously in my chest.

"Don't, *'Hannah'* me," she barks, not bothering to stop, but walks right past me. Her bag scrapes against the pavement, her feet moving faster away from me.

"Hannah, stop," I order, and her steps slow. Hannah's stubborn but secretly loves following my orders.

She stops, whipping around, her hair swinging in an arch behind her. "I'm fucking mad at you," she spits.

"I know, baby."

She scoffs, rolling her gorgeous eyes at me. "Sure, you fucking know," she mumbles, tears beginning to overflow and stream down her cheeks.

"I know," I start, "because I'm mad at me too."

"Are you, Anson? Really? Please tell me because you haven't been able to answer the goddamn phone!" She flings her arms out, her face reddening in anger. "You left without a word, took the blame for everything, and then ignored me." Her voice drops, aware that other people are walking along the docks. "So, please, tell me how *you're* the angry one in this scenario."

"I love you." The words fall from my lips and Hannah steps back as if I'd hit her. "I love you and I can't—couldn't—stay away."

"Well, it looks like you did a great job to me." Her voice drips with sarcasm, showcasing her hurt.

"I knew I couldn't have you from the moment I saw you. You were off-limits and I needed to stay away, but I couldn't. Everything about you draws me in," I explain. "I thought getting off the boat, cutting contact, was me righting that wrong. Fixing what I shouldn't have started."

"Oh great," her hands fly up around her, "now I'm a mistake. I'm done." She reaches for the handle of her bag, readying to walk away from me again, and I can't have that.

I reach out, grasping her wrist and pulling her to me. "Will you fucking listen for a minute?" Our faces are inches apart, both of us breathing heavily. "The only thing I regret is fighting the pull I have to you. All that time wasted..." My free hand drifts up to her jaw, cupping it gently.

Hannah breathes deeply, her eyes sliding closed. "You're an idiot," she says softly, making me chuckle.

"I never said I wasn't," I add, my thumb stroking along her lower lip.

"Did you mean what you said?" She asks, voice hesitant. "That you love me?"

A wide smile crosses my face, "Of course, baby. I've loved you since the moment I saw you. Did *you* mean it?" I ask, wanting to see if she's aware of those muttered words from that night. Her eyes pop open, sliding to mine.

"Yes, I remember." She smiles up at me, stealing the breath from my lungs. Her hands glide over my chest and cup the back of my neck, pulling me down to her. "I love you, Captain."

I don't hesitate to bring my lips to hers. She lets out a soft moan as we explore each other, our lips and tongues gliding together. I hold her close to me, reveling in the feel of her, the taste of her. Those haunting memories that kept me company while I was away from her are dull and faded compared to the real thing.

With great effort, I break our kiss, pressing our foreheads together as I fight to control my body's urge to take her against the nearest wall.

"Is that for me?" She steps back and reaches for the stuffed animal that I've somehow managed to keep ahold of, its body dangling as I hold it from a tentacle. She takes it from me, her eyes brimming with newfound tears.

"I remembered how much you love Henry, I thought you'd like one from me. An apology gift." She chuckles, hugging the plush toy to her chest.

"I love it," she mumbles. "Maybe they should only be for special occasions though," she laughs. My face must come across confused because she quickly adds, "If I get a Squishmallow every time you mess up, I think I'll run out of room."

Chuckling, I wrap an arm around her waist and pull her close, kissing her temple. "C'mon, baby. Let's get out of here."

Hannah looks up at me, her blue eyes gleaming in the sunlight. "Yes, Captain."

Epilogue

Two Years Later

Hannah

I bounce on the balls of my feet at the edge of the dock waiting for the ship to come into view. The wind whips through my hair, threatening to pull me backward, but nothing could pry my feet from this dock.

People walk up and down the docks, the water of the Mediterranean reflecting the sun's rays.

In two years, I've worked my way up from third stew to chief stew and I've never looked back. Including not going back to work on the *Siren*. It was fun while it lasted, but there are too many memories, both good and bad, that haunts me whenever I think about it.

Blocking the sun with my hand, I look to the horizon seeing the familiar outline of the boat I'm waiting on: *The Hannah*. I can't help the cringe that crosses my face anytime I think of the corny name, but Anson wouldn't budge.

"You and this boat are the only things I need," he said when he first told me. "My two greatest adventures share the same name."

Talk about romance.

The first few months after leaving the *Siren* were rough. I had a job as a stewardess, and he had his goal of owning a boat. It killed us both to have to spend so much time apart, but we've gotten into a routine.

When I'm on charter, he's out on the boat. When I'm off charter, he picks me up and we have an adventure.

I can have my cake and eat it too. At least, I think that's how the phrase goes.

I watch as he gets closer to the dock, excitement thrumming through me. It's been six long weeks on charter and I'm ready for my man.

There are times that he docks at the same dock as the boat I'm working on and on nights off, I manage to sneak away. With permission from the boat's captain, of course.

The Hannah sweeps over to the dock, its engine kicking up silt from the harbor floor. When all the lines are tied down and the engine shut off, I take off running.

Anson's head pops over the side, his blond hair shining in the sun. He's shaved off the scruff that was steadily turning gray, choosing to be clean-shaven instead. I don't mind, he always looks good to me. His face breaks out into a breathtaking smile that threatens to have my legs crumpling beneath me.

His feet thud against the wood of the dock moments before I crash into him. His strong arms wrap around me, lifting me off the ground and swinging me in a circle.

God, I've missed him.

He sets me down on my feet moments before planting his lips on mine. I moan, cupping his face in my hands before linking them around his neck. Strong hands lift me up and I wrap my legs around his hips.

"Hey, baby," he croons against my mouth, his hands flexing against my hips. "Miss me?"

"You know I did," I say, before pulling his lips back to mine.

Every bed without him in it feels empty, which makes it near impossible to sleep. Henry and Blue help, my two favorite

Squishmallows clutched against my chest every night. But they don't compare to the real thing.

Anson sets me down on my feet, reaching for my luggage with one hand and holding the other out for me.

My ring glints in the sunlight as Anson lifts my hand to his lips, kissing my ring finger softly.

He told me for months leading up to his proposal that he was going to marry me, but he kept me on my toes. When the time came, he kept it simple. He slipped the ring on my finger while I was cuddled against him in our bed, whispering the words he'd been teasing me with for months.

This was the last charter before we get married in two weeks. My mom flies into Greece next week to help with the setup and we couldn't be more excited.

Anson and I will be getting married on the deck of our ship, our relationship coming full circle.

We've traveled all over the world together, but nothing will top becoming his wife. And that, I think, is going to be the greatest adventure of all.

Thanks For Reading

Thank you for reading *Yes, Captain*!

I've been a lover of *Below Deck* for years and this book was so much fun for me to write! If you're an avid watcher of the show like myself, you might have noticed some nods to my favorite cast members. I just *had* to make my female main character's name Hannah— there was no other option in my mind.

I hope you enjoyed Hannah and Anson's story and fell in love with their crew members because I know I did. There's at least one crew member that I'd love to create a story around, so it's possible that I could turn this into a series... We'll have to wait and see.

If this is the first of my books that you've read and want to read more, check out the completed Claiming Her Series[1] that follows the Williams siblings. Each book follows a sibling and their love connections.

If you're looking for small-town spicy romcoms, check out The Rose Prairie Series[2]. I'm loving this small town and look forward to adding more storylines.

If you could, please take a moment to rate and review on Amazon, Goodreads, Instagram, or wherever you post reviews. As an indie author, ratings and reviews are the best way of

---

1. https://www.amazon.com/dp/
   B0BJCM3QPR?binding=kindle_edition&ref_=ast_author_bsi
2. https://www.amazon.com/gp/product/
   B0BS273PS2?ref_=dbs_p_pwh_rwt_anx_b_lnk&storeType=ebooks

getting my work out there for other people to read. A little goes a long way!

Don't forget to follow me on Instagram @authorsierrashipley [3] and sign up for my newsletter[4] to get freebies and see more details about my coming books!

Thank you for your support!

Until next time,

Sierra

---

3.   https://instagram.com/authorsierrashipley?igshid=YmMyMTA2M2Y=

4.   https://mailchi.mp/db7893726a2a/sierra-shipley-newsletter-sign-up-page

About the Author

Sierra Shipley is a born and raised Midwest girl. She spends her days with her lovable rescue pup, Trip, who constantly wants all the cuddles. Her ideal day is spent drinking coffee, reading, and dreaming.

Sierra has always wanted the romance she's read in books. Pair that with an active imagination and a love of creativity, and you get a writer!

Her goal is to create steamy, romantic stories with characters that people can relate to.

www.ingramcontent.com/pod-product-compliance
Lightning Source LLC
Chambersburg PA
CBHW030349180626
46812CB00007B/2813